Book 1 The Garden of lost Souls

The Grand Coward

Craig E. Hays

Dedicated to my parents who taught me how to be the man I am today

.

CONTENTS

ACKNOWLEDGMENTS

I greatly appreciate my friends, Brandon, Mike, and Tonia for taking the time to read through this book.

I am grateful to the company proofreadingandeditingservices.com for completing this project in such a short period of time.

PROLOGUE

It had been decades since anyone had set foot in this particular part of the world. Yes, it had been a very long time since anyone had ever dared enter this part of the world, except for those few that had made their home here. In the midst of this vast marsh, a fortress had been built. In the center of this fortress sat a single stone throne carved with little care and ordained with nothing more than vines and moss. A man sat perched on this throne. His body looked like a young man's, yet his posture was that of a man being crushed by all the woes of the world. It was as if his very shoulders held up not only the world but also the heavens. Motionless, he sat, eyes closed, appearing as if he were dead.

Clangs rang out through the fortress coupled with the grunts and groans of the two men who sparred before their master. One of the men wore a shield on both forearms. He danced around the room as he blocked the attacks of his partner, the other carrying no shield but a sword in each hand. His accuracy with each left the other man very little room for error when blocking a connecting slash or thrust. Both men gave no ground to the other, their smiles covered their faces ear to ear, looking like two young schoolboys playing with sticks and lids.

Standing not far from the two, in the center of the room, was a woman of beauty yet holding a presence of a battle-hardened warrior. The woman barked orders at the pair of sparring boys, critiquing their movements as they danced around each other. Her words, though harsh, held a hint of motherly caring. Her commanding words sometimes gave way to concern and worry as one of the men moved slower than she would have liked. The halberd she carried gleamed in the light that flickering light around the room from torches that lined the walls. Her hair moved back and forth ever so slightly in rhythm with the hot breath that came from behind her.

That breath was hot and damp yet somehow soothing. The rhythmic inhale and exhale of the beast that lay at the right of the man on the throne. Slightly larger than a horse and covered in white fur, small patches of brown appeared randomly across the great beast. Its great head had the appearance of a large dog, yet the fangs that lined the jaws of this beast suggested something different. Spikes protruded from either side of the beast's torso and along its spine with a single blade at the tip of the tail. Atop the beast lay a small figure of another woman. This one smaller than the last by more than a few inches.

This tiny woman lay on top of the beast with whimsical playfulness, rolling back and forth, poking the creature below her. Her dark hair matted down from the moisture dripping from the walls and ceiling of this fortress. Every once in a while, a small light of black and purple color shot up away from the woman, sending her in to a small fit of delight each time. Two daggers hang from the hips of this woman, each one black as an abyss, curved at the ends. She pointed one childlike finger at the man across the room who sat on the ruins of a once-grand statue, sending a small orb of swirling black and purple light at him.

The man did nothing more than let out a quick snort, causing the small orb of light to disappear. The man slouching upon the statue was of average build, covered with hardened muscle from years of training, wearing nothing more than a pair of shorts and a single plate of armor on his left shoulder, leaving countless scars open to the world. He simply sat watching the two young men spar in the center of the room, almost annoyed by their childish enthusiasm. He, along with all the others, seemed unbothered by the drops of water constantly forming and falling from the ceiling of the fortress. The humidity of the marsh condensing on the cold stone of the floors, walls, and ceilings formed puddles and an almost endless amount of water drops that fell echoing throughout the corridors of the vast fortress.

It wasn't a loud crash or boom that grabbed the attention of all those in the room, nor was it a scream or yell. No, it was nothing more than a sigh. A simple sigh lasting only for a fraction of a second. So quiet that it didn't cause even the slightest of echoes in the fortress. In that moment though, it was almost as if all of time stopped. The rain hung in midair; drops ready to fall simply hung with eager anticipation, as if waiting for permission. All eyes stared at the man on the throne and the source of the sigh.

The grins of the two men were somehow bigger than they were before, their eyes hungry to see what would happen next. Every inch of their muscles were tense and ready to move with explosive energy at a moment's notice. The woman who had been watching over them now turned to look at the man on the throne. A look of frustration and concern covered her face. Not the concern that you would get from danger but the kind you get when something doesn't go as planned.

The beast's eyes were now open; it didn't move or stir for fear of crushing the small woman on its great back. It stared intently at the man on the throne, holding its breath. The woman who had been lying on the beast's back now sat on her knees, trembling in anticipation, looking much like a small child at an amusement park.

Her eyes were wide, darting from the entrance to the room and to the man on the throne.

The man on the throne began moving slowly. His head rose from the hand that once supported it. Still it seemed as though his head itself weighed more than any man or woman could carry. His neck cracked and popped as he brought his head up. His voice carried throughout the hall as he spoke, raspy at first, ending with a hint of mischief.

"It would seem as though we have guests . . . I think we should show our hospitality and go and greet them." His eyes flashed open at the end of his statement, and a glow of red-and-black swirling light emanated from them, casting a menacing glow across the face of the man, multiplying the aura of the grin that now spread across his face.

It took but a second for the two men who were once sparring to dash from the room, saying nothing at first; but as they entered the corridors of the fortress, the laughter of the two echoed off the walls. The woman, who once stood chastising the two, simply shook her head and, with a sigh, set off in the same direction.

As the captain and her guards passed through the brush, it seemed to them as though a path had been cleared leading to the fortress that was built at the center of this marshland. Stories had been told to all of them when they were kids about the things that lurked in the bushes and waters of this part of the world. Warnings that were meant to last them their entire lives. Warnings to keep them from entering here, entering this place of malice and hatred.

The captain herself didn't fear these rumors, nor did she fear this land or the things that may hide just out of sight. The heaviness of her feet weighed down not only by her armor but by the mud that clung to her feet. Her determination was the reason she was given this assignment, and she would not fail her commanders. No, the trust that they had placed on her would not be misplaced; she would find him, and she would deliver the message that she had been charged with delivering. The only thought in her mind was keeping the fortress in sight. So long as she could see her destination, she would move forward until she finally reached her goal.

Her thoughts of reaching that goal were sent to the back of her mind as she stepped out into a small clearing, stopping dead in her tracks, causing the guards behind her to swear as they did all they could to avoid falling on their captain. She did not move, though; she barely even paid attention to the men around her. The only thing she could see was the figure of the woman standing before her.

The woman was a few inches shorter than the captain herself, standing maybe five feet five inches tall. Her straight hair moved whimsically in the light breeze, almost like that of a wheat field in the open plains. The light-brown color of her hair adding to this picture. Her arms were toned by the obvious use of the halberd she carried at her side. Everything about this woman screamed in the captain's mind that she was not someone to take lightly, yet her stance was carefree, almost annoyed by the presence of the captain and her guards.

"Who are you?" The woman's voice was stern, almost insulting, her eyes never leaving the gaze of the captain. One blue and one green, almost hypnotizing, stabbed at the captain's mind, probing for a hint of deceit in the captain's words. The woman's halberd glistened in the light as she spoke.

"I am Captain Anastasia from the city the Garden of Lost Souls. I am here to speak to a man named Kravin. If you know where I can find this man, then I would appreciate it. If not, can you point me to an easier route to that fortress?" Anastasia pointed toward the fortress as she spoke. "If you cannot do either of these two things, then I would appreciate it even more if you would please leave me and my men alone so we can continue." Anastasia returned the gaze of the woman across from her, hoping that the words she had chosen were not too offensive.

"Oh, you want Kravin, huh? And what exactly is it that you want with him? What does an illustrious captain of the guard from the *great city* Garden of Lost Souls want from the horrible and evil Kravin? Have you come to capture him? Slay him maybe?" A smirk dawned the mouth of the woman with the halberd as she leaned slightly forward. "Maybe you seek to be the mother of his children?"

Anastasia and her guards were startled as laughter erupted from either side of them. It lasted for but a moment, the guards remembering the training drilled into them quickly: form a circle around the captain ready to defend her with their lives. Anastasia herself never once looked away from the woman standing across the clearing, trusting her men fully with her own life.

The laughter though only increased as the two sparring partners stepped out of the marsh into the view of Anastasia and her guards. "Man, JP, can you believe this shit? This bitch actually thinks these guys can do something." The man's laughter was loud and full of pride.

"Yeah, it's pretty funny. She wouldn't be so confident standing there like that if she had a clue." The man wielding the two shields stood almost a head taller than the guards. Sweat beaded up and ran down off his bald head. Yet he stood there, cocky and imposing, allowing the guards to contemplate the situation they were in.

"Hey, Cher, what do you think? Can JP and I here have some fun with these guys?" The other man holding the two swords seemed almost the opposite. Although standing almost a head shorter than the guards, his presence was on par with the larger man's. His hair matted to his head, short yet still very thick. He swung his sword leisurely at the guards, mocking them, showing them he felt they posed no threat to any of them.

"Please, we have no intentions of fighting. We simply want to speak with Kravin," Anastasia said, still returning the gaze of the woman called Cher. Stilling her mind, Anastasia began creating a plan of attack in order to dispatch the three warriors that now stood in their way.

"Well, hun, it is all well and good that you want to complete your duty as a *captain* of the guard, but what would you say if I told you you're not going to be speaking to anyone ever again let alone Kravin?" A beam of light reflected from the blade of Cher's halberd shined in the eyes of Anastasia, causing her to blink for only a moment; but in that moment, the woman Cher closed the gap between them. The great blade of the woman's halberd stopped only fractions of an inch from the throat of Anastasia and what would have been a deadly strike.

The woman held her halberd position between the two men that stood between her and Anastasia. It was clear to Anastasia that the strike that would end her life would be followed by strikes to the two men that stood on either side of the woman's weapon. Neither of the men would be able to do anything to prevent the strikes that would take their lives and that of Anastasia.

The two men that stood on the sides of the group of guards began to circle like a pack of jackals, waiting for the cue to strike and satisfy their thirst for blood. Anastasia finally realized along with her men just how serious their situation truly was. These three warriors not only appeared to be vastly more experienced than herself and the guards with her, but they emanated a presence of overwhelming danger—a presence so great that Anastasia must use all her will to keep herself composed, ignoring the churning of her stomach. Her men, on the other hand, moved closer to their captain, tightening their ranks.

Anastasia and her men, though trained to die for their mission, could think of nothing more than running. Quickly, she and her guards scanned their surroundings, looking for an opening to escape from these three warriors. Sadly, Anastasia realized that there was none. The woman who seemed to be the superior of the three stood unyielding in front of them like a mountain. The two men circling them, grinning from ear to ear, moved nimbly as if floating. Anastasia knew that there was no chance of escape. All she and her men could do now was die fighting. With that realization, her hand moved to her sword hilt with precision and speed.

"Dumb" was the only word spoken from any of them. Cher, shifting her weight forward on her feet, began the thrust that would take the life of Anastasia. It would quickly continue into a series of strikes that would make short work for the two men on either side of her. From the moment Anastasia opened her eyes to the moment she reached for her sword seemed to take days but, in truth, it happened so quickly it was almost simultaneous. All that thought, preparation, and analysis that led up to Anastasia's decision to fight was shattered though.

A deafening roar erupted from the distance. Anastasia, facing the fortress, could tell that whatever it was that caused it was somewhere in that fortress. Cher's momentum was halted instantly. The two men circling the guards both stopped, stood straight up, and were surprised by what just happened, their ravenous hunger no longer apparent, instead looking as though they had just been punished by an elder.

Cher's smirk left her face and was replaced by the annoyed look she held at the beginning of the encounter with Anastasia. "Well, it would seem I was wrong, Captain, you will get to speak to someone again. Follow me and the boys. We will lead you to the fortress." Cher spun on her heels with a grace Anastasia had not expected and began walking.

The two men who once looked as though they wanted to feast on Anastasia and her guards leapt into the air, clearing the entire company with no more effort than a child playing hopscotch. "Hurry up, we don't have all day." The smaller man walked backward, again taunting the guards, but his smile was missing; instead, his expression was only of anger.

It took Anastasia only a moment to bark orders at her men to follow, knowing full well that whatever just happened, that roar just saved their lives. Anastasia wasn't sure what would happen next and if she should put her and the lives of her men in the hands of these three, but it was the only thing she could do at this moment. As they walked, she began to think out how they should handle the coming journey and, more importantly, how to keep them safe without provoking their newly found guides.

CHAPTER 1

They entered the fortress late in the afternoon, which was one of many things that set Anastasia's senses on high alert. She had seen the fortress as they moved through the marsh, and with all her training, she knew that there was no way that they should have been able to cover that much ground in such a short amount of time. What she had planned to be two days' travel at least had turned into a five-hour march. Yet here they were entering the fortress that was their goal. In a few short minutes, she would be able to find the man named Kravin and complete her mission.

She could not help but notice how much moisture was in the air as they passed through the short length of corridors. It was almost as if the whole fortress had been flooded. Puddles as deep as her ankles hid sharp stones and jagged edges. Water dripped constantly from the ceiling, sending shivers down her back as it found its way inside her armor through various openings. It was all she could do to keep her will strong. It wasn't just the area the fortress was built in or the moisture that hung in the air like a cloud and ran down every wall. It was an overwhelming presence that tugged at her will to keep moving.

It wasn't just her; she noticed even her men, some of whom had seen countless battles with the Oritha, seemed unsettled by this place. Their eyes darted down every corridor, and their hands never strayed more than an inch from their swords. The group was small and, in the presence of whatever was in this fortress, seemed to make them appear like ants. The other thing that kept nagging at her was the fact that as they got closer to their destination, the three who had guided them here seemed to change. Their moods, once annoyed and angered by the presence of Anastasia and her men, now seemed anxious and rowdy. The woman was the only exception; her mood, though slightly more relaxed than it had been prior to entering the fortress, still seemed stressed and aggravated.

Anastasia wondered if the woman knew what her mission was and perhaps she wanted to prevent Anastasia from completing it. Whatever this woman's ideas may be,

Anastasia would not let her get in the way of her mission. If it had to come to a fight, Anastasia would ready herself for the fight of her life. What she did not know was that this fight would not be with the woman who had led her here but with the man she was about to meet.

The corridors for the most part were dimly lit, which, paired with the water-logged floor, Anastasia could only compare it to walking on a sheet of ice in pitch-black. More than a few times, her men had to help each other up or prevent each other from falling as they marched through the narrow passages. Finally after what seemed to be an eternity of walking through these corridors, Anastasia could see that the corridor finally stopped at a room.

Anastasia quickly tried to recall the twists and turns they had taken to get to this part of the fortress, but it suddenly occurred to her just how well this fortress was built. Stopping at the exit of the corridor, she turned around as if looking at her men; but in reality, she was scanning the corridor. Her eyes twitched slightly, realizing her memory had not failed her but the opposite.

She remembered almost every part of the corridors and hallways they had passed through and none of them had any distinguishing markings. Every one of them looked exactly like the last, and with the dim lighting, any markings that would be able to give them a sense of direction could not be seen. Add on the slippery walls and floors, there would be no way that her group could hope to leave this place with any type of speed. On the contrary, the more she analyzed the route and the passages, the more certain she became: if they were to enter these corridors alone, if those who dwelled here did not kill them, they would simply wait for them to die. It was a labyrinth, one that you could not see your way through and would never be able to walk with firm steps. It seemed their only hope was to enter the room ahead and pray that their mission could be completed.

Spinning on her heel without thinking, Anastasia nearly fell but caught herself on the doorway of the room. A roar of laughter echoed up from the corridor from behind her as the two men who had been following them weaved their way in between her men.

"Geez, it must have been pure luck you guys made it this far." The smaller of the two men jumped around Anastasia to stand in the dim light of the room. His grin was menacing as always, yet something in his eyes was playful, as if he had found a new toy and was eager to play with it. "OK, so we brought them here. Now what?" He looked away from Anastasia as he spoke, but something about him still held her gaze.

As Anastasia looked at the man who had been tormenting them, she could not pinpoint just what held her gaze, keeping her from looking away. Her eyes scanned every inch of the man, trying to find what it was that distinguished him so. His hair was short almost bald yet still covered all of his head. His face was thin and his eyes were dark. Surprisingly, the man had a tan, which slightly perplexed Anastasia because in her time here, she thought it impossible to get that much sun. The armor he wore was light, if anything sloppily worn, sliding and shifting on his arms and shoulders as he walked. The swords, however, seemed to be a point of pride for him. She had noticed earlier during their travel here that he would unconsciously touch them and rub the hilts.

Yet even, so they had no signs of wear. The blades slapped against his thighs as he walked and gleamed in the light. There was no question that those blades were keen enough to cut a man in two. Aside from the swords and the disheveled look of his armor, there was nothing about this man that should hold her gaze for as long as it did. With all her analyzing, it was a slight growl from her left that finally drew her gaze away from the man.

Finally stepping all the way into the massive room, Anastasia stared at what she thought was the source of the growl. She stared at a beast the size of a horse yet almost doglike in appearance. The only thing that truly set it apart was the fangs in its muzzle and the spikes running down its sides and back. She and her men stared at the creature for a moment when again the growl drew her attention away.

Anastasia quickly scanned the room looking for the source of the growl, yet she found nothing. It wasn't until she started to look back at the beast that she finally noticed him. She had looked over the man who sat next to the beast. As she looked at him, it seemed as if he melded with the stone throne. His face was pale, matching the water-worn gray stone of the throne.

His hair was gray like old newspaper, spiked in the front then gradually lying down in the back. Though he seemed small in the large throne he sat in, she could tell that he was of average build, yet tall. He wore clothing made of black threads highlighted in areas with a rich purple and orange. His posture was as if he alone held the world in the palm of his hands, reigning over everything he could touch. With head held high and shoulders back, he glared at her with interest and curiosity.

It wasn't until their eyes finally met that she saw the expression on his face in detail. It was also the moment she realized just what the ominous presence was that seemed to beat through this fortress like blood. His expression was gentle, yet his eyes were hard and untrusting, seeming to look right into the soul of Anastasia.

"Come now, girl, you need to relax a bit, such a serious expression will cause you wrinkles." His smile was warm, yet again, his eyes seemed to disagree with the rest of his expression. "Don't worry. As long as you keep those useless weapons at your side, none of us will cause you any harm." Finally to the relief of Anastasia his eyes matched the expression on his face. One that wasn't hard and daunting but almost pleading, but only for a second.

"My lord, my name is Captain Anastasia Ladin of the Garden of lost Souls city guard. My men and I are on a mission to deliver a message to a man by the name of Kravin. I was told that once we reached this fortress, we would be able to find this man. If you could please give us any information about this man and where we may find him, it would be greatly appreciated, and we will be on our way." Anastasia bowed deeply more to avert her eyes from this man's gaze than to conform to formalities.

"Well, I see that some of you still have some manners in that city, aye, girl? Yet tell me, what would the illustrious city Garden of Lost Souls want with Kravin?" For the first time, the man who sat on the throne moved. Leaning forward, resting his elbows on his knees, and clasping his hands, he looked at Anastasia intently as if challenging her.

"My lord, I was charged with delivering a message to Kravin and only Kravin. I do not wish to offend you, but I cannot allow anyone other than him to hear my message. Please forgive me if you find this insulting." Again, Anastasia bowed, trying to avert her gaze from the man who sat in the throne. She needed these few seconds to gather her wits and think of what she should say next.

A smirk appeared across the face of the man on the throne. "So let me get this straight. You came to my fortress seeking help to find Kravin. Yet you are unwilling to tell me what it is you need this man for other than to deliver a message?" He raised one eyebrow as if curious to see how Anastasia would react to this line of questioning.

"Again, my lord, I cannot tell you any more than I already have." Anastasia prayed that her response would not be taken as an insult, yet she knew already that this man had set a trap for her. She also knew she had no other option but to step right into his trap.

The face of the man who sat before Anastasia seemed amused by her response, allowing a smirk to cross his face. Leaning back into the throne, the man took a moment simply looking at Anastasia before responding. "Well, I must say you get points for your honesty and a few more for being so dedicated to your mission. Although you do realize what you just said not only cost you your life but the lives of your men as well, don't you, girl?" The man sat as if he had just played a game with her and won.

Hearing this, Anastasia's hand flashed to the hilt of her sword. Her men, reacting in the same manner, began to move toward their captain. In the same instant, Anastasia watched as the beast lying next to the throne stood tossing what seemed to be a small girl off to the floor in shock. Its spikes no longer flat on its back but stood up like barbs. The beast's jowls pulled back, showing even larger amounts of razor-like fangs. A growl erupted from the beast, and this time, Anastasia knew it was the beast that this growl came from.

"ENOUGH!" The man's voice boomed through the halls, as if emanating not only from him but from the very structure itself. The deafening roar sent Anastasia and her men to their knees, stunned by the power of his voice. The man stood from his throne for the first time with more grace than anyone she had ever seen. As he walked toward her, it seemed as though his feet barely touched the earth.

The man bent over and cupped Anastasia's chin, slowly picking her up from the ground. Anastasia was in awe as this man picked her up with a single hand as if she weighed no more than a sheet of paper. More astonishing that he could do so without causing her pain. Once she stood on her own, the man looked deep into her eyes as if searching for something.

"Allow me to introduce myself. I am Kravin, the man you seek. Welcome to my home, girl, and again we wish you no harm. I apologize for the ludicrous game I played, but I was curious as to just how far you would go to complete your mission."

"You? You're Kravin. Former commander of the Garden of Lost Souls?" Anastasia could do nothing to hide the shock. She looked the man from head to toe for the first time and could barely believe his words. His clothes were loose and almost ragged; he wore no weapon, no armor, and nothing suggesting he was the commander spoken of in story.

"First off, let's get a few things straight, girl. The first thing is, my name is Kravin, not 'my lord'. The second is, I have not worn the crest of the Garden of Lost Souls. In quite some time now. So please keep it informal. To be honest, I am seriously bored of this formality crap anyway." Kravin returned to his throne, slouching, leaning his head upon his right shoulder. "Now, how about you go ahead and deliver that amazingly important message so you can be on your way and I can get back to what I was doing."

Anastasia looked at the man Kravin. Her mind was jumbled, and nothing had prepared her for this. Her thoughts raced jumping from one though to another, questioning this man's words. How could this man be the great Kravin? After a moment, she managed to calm her thoughts and compose herself so that she could deliver the message she was charged with, but first she must make sure this was truly the man she was seeking. "I am sorry, Kravin, I cannot simply take your words at face value. Do you have any proof as to what you say is true? If you can prove that you are not lying, then and only then can I tell you the message."

"Fine then, come here and take my hand, girl." Kravin sat forward once again, yet this time it was almost like a chore for the man. Holding out his hand, pale and slightly bony, with a slight motion. His nails trimmer and clean looked like glass.

Hesitantly, Anastasia moved forward, taking Kravin's hand. She regretted this fact almost immediately though as a flood of images entered her mind. Images of the man standing with the commanders of the city, speaking with the citizens, even helping to construct parts of the city itself, flashed through her mind. Images of war. Images that turned her stomach. Experiences that sent chills down her spine all spun a short story of this man's past in her mind. Just as quickly as the images appeared they disappeared as Kravin released her hand and sat back into the throne once more.

"Well, girl, if that wasn't enough to prove what I say is true, then I would appreciate it if you get out of my home." His eyes were stern and menacing once again, almost daring her to challenge what he had just shown her.

Again, Anastasia found herself fighting to compose herself from the presence of this man. As she looked upon Kravin, her eyes no longer shone brightly with determination; instead they were filled with tears. Quickly, she wiped away those tears and looked at Kravin for the first time, recognizing him as the man she was sent to speak with.

CHAPTER 2

"Kravin, I'm sorry that I doubted you, and yes, that was more than enough to prove what you say is true. You already know who I am and where I came from, so I am just going to tell you what I have to say." Anastasia took a step forward, and again, the beast, which calmed, down let out a growl but stayed sitting next to the throne. "Kravin, the Garden is under siege by the Oritha. Commander Destriga and Commander Bear both sent me to come and find you and ask you. Kravin, please help the Garden. According to the commanders, you are the only man who can help us now!" Anastasia allowed her emotions to take control as she spoke, thinking of the loved ones that she and her men left behind as they went on this mission.

Kravin, who at first seemed uninterested in the message Anastasia was delivering, quickly turned his eye upon her as she asked him for help. His glare was piecing and seemed almost to cause Anastasia pain without touching her. His lips curled and twitched as he sat forward, his eyes never leaving hers. "You really think that I would help that wretched city?" Kravin stood in a flash and moved toward Anastasia, the sheer power of his presence driving her and her men backward. "NO! I will not come to the aid of that place, nor you. If you cannot defend yourself, then you have no right to exist." His words were cold and short, his glare, again, never leaving Anastasia.

Anastasia's heart sank as she heard these words. Her unyielding determination to complete her mission had all been for nothing. Her body trembled and her thoughts raced. What could she say to this man to change his mind. How could she plead for the help her home so desperately needed? Closing her eyes tightly, she combed her thoughts for something; maybe one of the memories he had shared with her could give her the one piece of information she needed to compel this man to help. Seconds went by; Anastasia, eyes closed and trembling, searched her thoughts. Slowly, the trembling subsided; and when she spoke, it was not pleading but instead demanding. "You helped create that *wretched* city. You helped create my home and gave my family a place to live, and now you say you will not help?" She tried as hard as she could to return the glare that Kravin had given her.

A menacing laugh echoed through the room, startling Anastasia as she scanned the room for the source. It took a second, but finally, she found the source of the laugh. In the shadows of one the pillars that supported the ceiling of this great room stood the man who had laughed at her determination. His arms folded in front of him, his hair was slightly long, stopping at his shoulders. He didn't move but simply stared at the floor in front of him as if nothing that was happening interested him. "I wouldn't provoke my brother, girl. You may not like what you see." His voice was deep and quite.

"YOU ENTER MY HOME WITH WEAPONS, CALL ME A LIAR, THEN TRY TO INTIMIDATE ME INTO HELPING YOU." Kravin's eyes flared with energy, swirling and flashing out in all directions. "Ta, please show these fools the door, get them home." Kravin never took his eyes from Anastasia as he spoke. The small girl who had been on the beast jumped and giggled as she darted forward toward the guards', eager to perform the task she was given.

The small woman began swirling her hands in front of her, leaving a trail of energy similar to that which erupted from Kravin's eyes. After a second, the energy formed a portal and swirled mesmerizingly in the center of the room behind Anastasia and her men. "Right this way, weaklings. My bro says it's time for you to go." Her high-pitched giggle was insulting and menacing at the same time.

Anastasia had turned and watched as this small woman created the portal, but now she turned to face Kravin, hoping to get one last word in to convince him to help the city. What she did instead surprised even her. She had expected that same glare from Kravin but instead was met not just with the glare but Kravin standing inches from her. He had bent over, slightly putting him almost nose to nose with her. Instantly, her knees had buckled, and she fell to the floor.

After the initial shock had worn off, she began to pick herself up off the floor and turned to her men, who too were shocked by just how close he had gotten. She didn't say a word as she marched to the portal that she hoped would take them outside this fortress. She did everything she could to keep herself composed; she would not show any more weakness to these people than she already had. Never in all her years of service had anyone come that close without her even hearing them. *No breath* was the one thing that seemed to scream in the back of her mind; no—that close, she should have been able to feel his breath, yet there was none. As her group entered the portal, Anastasia heard but one thing, the girl who had opened the portal for them throwing one final insult "Have a nice day, and thanks for coming!"

After the captain and her men had entered the room, the small woman closed the portal behind them. Spinning with delight, she danced to a music no one else could hear back toward the large beast next to the throne but stopped short as she caught view of Kravin. She, like everyone else in the room, knew all too well what this particular look meant. Her whimsical delight turned to curiosity at the thought of what was to come and just what kind of action Kravin would be taking.

Kravin had turned his back on the group and moved toward his throne; again, it seemed as if the weight of the world had fallen upon his shoulders. His movements that seemed so quick and precise were now sluggish; his feet shuffled across the floor as he moved. His head hung low, deep in thought. Seeing this, Cher spoke first, knowing what it was that Kravin had in mind.

"You can't be serious. You made the decision to leave that place and now you want to go back?" Her tone was accusing and harsh; she made it very clear that she did not agree with the thoughts of Kravin. Kravin, however, did not acknowledge her at first; his back seemed like a wall preventing her voice from reaching him. "KRAVIN! You cannot do this, we followed you here to help you and now you want to throw it all away?"

Kravin slammed his hands on the arms of his throne, sending cracks spider-webbing throughout it. His voice was low and menacing when he spoke; it echoed from every wall and tunnel within the fortress, making it very clear that his decision will not be questioned. "You of everyone here know full well what my options are. If I do not go, then all these years have been nothing but a waste either way. I am going, dear sister. Whether you come or not is your decision, but I cannot just let that city fall."

The small woman squealed with delight and vanished; the two men who had accompanied Cher earlier again ran from the room down a corridor, their footsteps echoing and slowly fading. The other man who had stood in the shadows stepped forward with a *hmph*. He walked toward Cher, never looking at Kravin, his face was like stone. As he stepped next to Cher, he placed his hand on her shoulder and simply nodded as if to tell her that Kravin was right.

Cher huffed and turned her gaze to Kravin; her look was of scorn, yet her voice quivered with concern about the decision Kravin had made. "Well, if things get out of hand, don't think for a second that I won't do what I have to do to protect this family, Kravin. We all care about you, but I will not let this family get hurt because of you."

Kravin turned around, his gaze was light and thankful; a smile had crossed his mouth now. "My dearest sister, I love you as well and I would expect nothing less from you. You have spent so many years taking care of us like a mother, and I would never expect you to stop for any reason. Thank you for understanding and for caring." Kravin walked toward the center of the room to join Cher and the other man.

As Kravin joined the two in the center of the room, the small woman who had disappeared earlier reentered the room from a portal. Her grin was playful and full of sin; she quivered as she walked, not hiding the anticipation of what was to come. Again, the echo of footsteps came from one of the corridors as the two men entered the room, brimming with confidence, laughing and slapping each other on the back; it seemed as if they too were eager to see what their future held.

Kravin's tone was like he spoke to a child at this point. "Sis, if you would be so kind?" He turned not to Cher but to the small woman who seemed overly zealous of the situation at hand. She did not respond; instead she allowed a small squeak to escape her throat before waving her hand in front of them, creating yet another portal. "I hope this doesn't go to the front lines, sis, I would rather get a good idea of what is happening before we make any decision."

"Oh, come on, brother, don't get me wrong. I would love to do that, but I know you better than that. We will have a great view from where this goes." She giggled slightly when speaking to Kravin; it was almost like she was trying to hide her true intent, but her eyes told Kravin she was being honest.

Kravin stepped through the portal first; he hesitated for a split second before entering, but he hardened his gaze and moved forward. The man from the shadows looked at Cher and the small woman, slightly bowing and holding his hand out toward the portal. Cher returned his look and walked through; the small woman snorted at his chivalry then danced as she entered the portal. After the three men had stepped through the portal, it began to shrink and disappear but stopped and became large again. Kravin's hand emerged from the portal; he snapped his fingers and beckoned towards the portal. The beast huffed as it stood then trotted quickly to the portal, following its master.

CHAPTER 3

Anastasia stared in awe as she exited the portal; she had no idea that the people who she had just encountered had the kind of power that she had just witnessed. Like everyone else in the Garden, she had always been under the impression that the commanders Destriga and Bear were two of the most powerful people she would ever know of. The idea was shattered though after meeting those people—most of all, meeting Kravin. The thought of the man she was sent to speak to was all it took to send a shiver down her spine.

It took her a moment to regain her composure and really take a look around at her surroundings. Her men had already started fanning out to check their surroundings and make sure that they were in a safe place, but Anastasia already knew that everything was fine. She had played here many times in her youth and knew that the enemy forces had not spread this far. She also knew that they were not far from the entrance to the city.

"Captain, it seems like we are only a few hundred yards from the city. From the looks of it, probably somewhere around south east of the city." Her lieutenant stood at attention as he brought her the news of where they had been sent by the small woman.

"I know exactly where we are, Lieutenant, but thank you for the information. Our destination is fifty yards in that direction. Look for a tree with moss in the shape of a shield on it. That is the hidden entrance to the city." Anastasia pointed in the direction her men needed to travel. "Get the men and start moving. I will follow you in a moment. I want to check on something first." Anastasia stood and turned away from the man.

"Yes, ma'am!" The man saluted and walked quickly to gather the rest of the men and start their journey toward the entrance and, finally, a much-needed rest.

Anastasia stood looking into the distance with her back to her men as they started moving. It took everything she had to keep her composure so that her men would not know just how distraught she really was. She could not stop thinking about what had just happened and what it meant for the city she so loved. Thankfully, her will kept her tears from streaming down her face. She had to wait until after she could barely hear her men's movements in the distance. Finally, when she could no longer hear them, she crumpled to the ground, sobbing.

"Why, why wouldn't you help this city? We risked our lives to save our city, to find you, and you just turned your back and mocked us. It isn't worth helping a city that can't help itself! What kind of arrogant thinking is that?" Anastasia turned her head to the sky, her tears gleaming in the sunlight. "YOU BASTARD!" Realizing just what she had done, she looked around and listened, hoping that her men had not heard her.

It no longer mattered what had just happened was all she could think. She needed to get back to the city and tell Commander Bear and Commander Destriga that Kravin had refused to help them. After that, there was only one option, and that was to go back to the lines and do everything she could to defend the city she so dearly loved. Brushing the dirt from her body, Anastasia stood and began moving in the direction her men had starting moving.

Tracing the outline of the shield on the tree, it took only a second for the door to move and reveal the tunnel that would take her to the inter part of the city. She took one last look around before entering and was surprised to see all of her men standing just inside in the tunnel, waiting for the captain. She gave them a slight smile and simply walked past them moving toward the city, and her now weighing duty.

It took them only about an hour to reach the end of the tunnel. Anastasia ordered her men to go home and rest for now. "Enjoy the time you can with your families. Take this time to rest and make grand memories because tomorrow, we will be on the front lines once again, defending this city and our families." She, though, had one last thing she had to do before she too could get what little rest she could manage before heading out for the lines once again.

She saluted her men then turned and walked with stone-like determination toward the fortress that stood at the center of the city. She had no idea just how her commanders would take this message, but she hoped that they had some kind of plan B prepared. The city was quiet as usual at this time. As she walked forward, she found her mind slowly wandering to various memories of the city.

She passed over the bridge where that foolish boy stole a kiss from her for the first time; she chuckled, remembering the fact that in return, she had given him a swift kick to the groin. Then blushed slightly, remembering how she actually enjoyed the kiss though her reaction did not quite relay that. It seemed as if every corner of this city had some kind of memory attached to it, both good and bad. As she came to the great doors that lead into the fortress, she sighed and uttered a simple comment to herself. "No matter what, I will protect these people." With that, Anastasia pushed open the door and stepped inside.

Anastasia entered the room in which the commanders Destriga and Bear sat waiting for her. Both men sat on high-backed chairs at a large round table. Though the table held many chairs, only these two men were present. This had been the first time Anastasia had ever entered this room, and she was awed by it. The walls were scarred and scorched from top to bottom; even the ceiling held marks that hinted at great battles, stories she could only imagine. The only light in the room came from a large fire that oddly enough burned in the center of the table.

Anastasia looked rather closely at this, noticing that the large hole that contained the flames did not seem to have been part of the original construction but instead had been created later. She pondered the thought as to why someone would do such a horrid thing to such an amazing piece of the work. Every part of the table seemed adorned with some kind of ornate carving.

"Captain, I realize this is your first time being in this room, but we have more pressing matters at hand. Like what exactly did Kravin say? Of course that is assuming you completed your mission and did indeed find him?" The voice was low and booming, as would be expected from the man known as Commander Bear. His eyes stabbed at Anastasia like daggers, urging her to deliver her message as quickly as possible.

"My apologies, Commander, it has been a long journey, and I am starting to succumb to the fatigue." Anastasia saluted her commanders, quickly realizing just how casual she had been when entering the room.

"Well then, Captain that would seem to be all the more reason as to why you need to deliver your message as quickly as possible." Destriga too spoke condemningly towards the women, pushing her to give them her message and leave as quickly as possible.

"Commanders, I am sorry to report that the man Kravin you sent me to find has rejected our request for assistance." Anastasia trembled slightly, not knowing what to expect from her two commanders. The trembling stopped instantly as she watched in shock at how her commanders reacted.

Both men grin widely and nodded to each other. Both of them seemed as if some great miracle had just taken place right in front of them, yet Anastasia could not understand why. Her anger began to well up inside her at the sight of these two men who seemed delighted at the fact that the man who was supposed to save them had simply rejected her because they needed his help. Her anger took only a minute to get to the breaking point, and with that, she could no longer control herself.

"You fools, are you that tired? Didn't you hear what I just said? That pompous, arrogant bastard refused to help us simply because we need his help. You put so

he moved to leave the room, snapping his fingers. As he exited, the fire fizzled and went out.

CHAPTER 4

Kravin stepped out of the portal created by the small woman, finding himself standing atop a ridge, looking at his former home the Garden of lost Souls. "Ta, I must say you picked an amazing spot to bring us, thank you." His smile lasted only a second as he looked out upon the land that lay before him. The land that now was overrun with the beast known as the Oritha. These foul creatures were a bane to everything that existed in this world.

"What the . . . since when do those ugly things start traveling in such large numbers? I mean I know they might travel in packs around twenty or so, but never this many. Hell, how many do you think are down there?"

The man grasped the straps of his shields, giving them a good tug, ensuring that they were tight.

"It looks to be around fifty thousand, JP, and more beyond the forest line. Either that or something far worst." Kravin looked off in to the distance, past the fields around the city toward the pillars of smoke that were rising up from the forests beyond. As his companions followed his gaze, none of them showed signs of nervousness. Instead, the small woman called Ta began to dance in wonderment, and the man with the swords rubbed the hilts of his swords in anticipation.

"Well, bro, how about we get to this then. I for one have been starving for a good fight for years." The swordsman's voice quivered in excitement, his eyes moving quickly over the mass of Oritha in front of them, almost as if he were cutting a path through them.

"Not yet, Skinny. Tonight we wait. Tomorrow, we will see what happens in the battle between the city and those things. After that, we will act." Kravin's tone suggested that there would be no buts and that his decision was final. Hearing this, the others spread out amongst the trees and brush, securing the area and finding suitable places to rest for the night, all except the woman Cher and the other larger man.

"Well, brother, you got any plans?" The man never looked directly at Kravin. He simply stared off toward the field filled will Oritha, his arms folded, with a brooding look that seemed to always be upon his face. "Just to be clear, I am not talking about how you plan on handling them but how you plan on handling her."

A slight smile crossed Kravin's face as he responded. "The plan was very simple there, Dawg. Get in and finish this up before she ever comes around and finds out that I am here." Though he smiled when saying this, something in his voice told Dawg that this was not completely true. In reality, Dawg thought to himself that Kravin was more than likely hoping she would find out.

"Well, I will not lie, brother. I will kill any man you tell me to and all the Oritha in the world. However, I will not go near her, and you know that." With that final statement, Dawg turned and walked off in to the thick of trees and disappeared from view.

"Why do you feel it necessary to lie about it? We all know the reality of the situation. Hell, honestly, I think sometimes you lie not to us but to yourself. Yeah, know what, never mind. Pleasant dreams, brother." Cher walked to a nearby tree, laying her halberd next to her; she sat against the tree and began to fall asleep.

Kravin looked at Cher almost apologetically and began to rise up off the ground. Higher and higher he floated until he was on the top of the tree line; there, he stopped and began to speak only loud enough for him to hear. "It's been a long time, hasn't it, my old friend. Fifty years I have spent in that marsh wasteland trying to avoid you.

Yet now look at you, surrounded with these horrid creatures on the brink of destruction. What I do not get though is how is it that both Bear and Destriga are unable to protect you themselves. Well, do not worry. I will protect you, and I pray she does not have too much anger towards me." His gaze never moved from the city, his memory slowly etching an image of the city and the sun setting behind it.

The next morning, Cher awakened with a start, not fully used to sleeping against trees. It took her only a moment to realize where she was and remember why she was there. Standing, she took a look around, making sure that everything was fine and that she has not slept through anything. As usual, Kravin was awake and standing on the edge of the cliff, looking out into the distance at the city and the army that stood before it. JP and Skinny, tangled in a bush, snoring loudly, seemed like actual brothers. She smirked at the idea that in a few hours, these two men would be awake and in the middle of battle, their innocent looks all but forgotten.

As usual Ta, was nowhere to be found, more than likely off playing a sick game of cat and mouse with some poor animal. Dawg, as they call him, never stayed where anyone can easily see him, so she doesn't even think about it when she does not see him anywhere. "Ya know, sometimes I swear you never sleep, do you? Anyway, anything happen while we slept?"

"No." Kravin's tone is one of concentration. His eyes flashed back and forth across the field in front of them as he played out the coming battle in his mind. Like chess, the man tried to figure out the strategy of his enemy and tried to keep a few steps ahead of him in order to keep his losses at a minimum. It wasn't until the two men behind him woke in a ruckus that Kravin diverted his attention.

"What the—! Skinny, get your foot out of my mouth before I break it off!" JP grabbed Skinny by the ankle, tossing him off to the side. Skinny landed on his feet with catlike agility, smiling and laughing.

"Ah, come on, JP, it's just a little jam for your toast, bro. Not like you haven't had some before. Honestly, I thought you liked the flavor." He danced around JP kiddingly, taunting him at the same time. Both men began to wrestle, releasing tension from the coming battle. Both taunted each other and laughed until Ta entered the small clearing.

Ta, running full speed from one of her portals, charged at Kravin leaping on to his back. Kravin stood like a solid wall, never giving any hint that this small woman had just clung to his back. Ta rested her head on his shoulder, staring off at the mass of Oritha that waited for them.

"So when do we get to play?" Her voice quivered with excitement as she stared starry eyed at her enemy.

"I have not yet decided if you will be having any fun today, Ta." His tone was stern and unyielding.

"What! That's not fair! Why does everyone else get to have fun but I don't?" Ta pushed out her lower lip, pouting at the fact that Kravin won't be allowing her to fight in the battle.

"To bad, Ta, looks like you're stuck watching from the sidelines. Don't worry, I will kill a couple of them for you." Skinny made no attempt at hiding the sarcasm in his voice. His grin quickly twisted in pain. Ta created two portals just behind; her feet and kicked backward through the portal: one connecting with the groin of Skinny and the other to JP's chin.

"HEY! Why did you kick me, I didn't say a word!" JP, rubbing his jaw, stared at the small woman in disbelief, bewildered by the fact that she had just kicked him for what he felt was no reason at all.

"Hmph, don't you know? I'm a girl, which means guilt by association since you're his friend." Ta turned her nose to the air, adding to her point.

"Enough! I do realize you are all excited about what's going to happen, and I know that you are all pretty much crazy as well. Even so, stop acting like a bunch of kids at an amusement park. Also just to remind all of you, Kravin may still be here, but we all know he cannot give us any support. So remember, no matter how much trouble you get into in the battle, we are all on our own." Cher glared at each of them for a moment before turning back to the field and standing next to Kravin.

Kravin stood on the cliff, staring off into the distance, his expression never changing, never giving any hint to what he was thinking. Cher and Dawg knew though; the two of them knew exactly what was behind those great walls for Kravin and what he had left behind when he walked away. She looked at him for a second, pondering just what was exactly behind those cold eyes. Were there scenes of a great battle playing out, or had he finished those thoughts and moved on to thoughts of her warm embrace and beautiful smile?

"Brother, would you mind finding the others some breakfast? For some odd reason, I get the feeling that they would cause more harm if they were allowed to find their own breakfast." Kravin never moved when speaking to his brother.

"Sure." Dawg looked at the three almost as if they were a simple annoyance then walked off into the woods, making almost no noise. As he moved, it was as if the forest itself embraced him and the limbs and branches of the trees and brush moved to conceal him as he moved. Leaves blew out of his way as if giving him a path to walk.

It was then that Cher realized that Dawg had returned from his morning hunt. Dawg had been with Kravin since the beginning as had Bear and Destriga. Unlike the other two, Dawg was Kravin's brother by birth and not by choice, which was the case with Destriga and Bear. In their youth, the two fought constantly as normal brothers. The two had very distinct personalities that would clash at times, yet no matter what, it was common knowledge they would be there for each other no matter what happened. After the flare, after they had each gained the powers they currently possessed, it was amazing the tandem the two had developed.

Cher was always stunned at how well the two worked together. She had noted on several occasions how it seemed as if Kravin was the one in charge at all times, yet Dawg seemed to have the very same thoughts as Kravin. Many times Kravin needed only to look at Dawg for him to act. All the years the three of them had spent together, she still felt a small amount of awe when she would watch the two men work together. It was almost like twins, yet the age difference was four years.

It took Dawg only a few minutes to bring back a deer from the surrounding forest, his hands dripping with fresh blood as he carried their breakfast over his shoulder. He moved quickly, setting up a stand for the animal so that they could cook the deer. Dawg pushed two large branches into the ground and hung the deer between the two as if to start a fire underneath the animal, yet instead of setting wood under the animal, he simply looked at Cher. "Sis?" was all the man said as he waited for her to respond.

Cher knew what it was that Dawg was wanting, and without a word, she stepped forward and looked at the deer. Her eyes glowing red as she did, and slowly the meat of the deer began to darken and cook. Aside from gaining heightened physical abilities, Cher had also acquired the ability to heat anything she looked at. It took her only a few moments to bring the meat to an editable temperature. "All right, you three go ahead and eat. It's done." Without any hesitation, the three began to cut meat from the deer and devour it as if they had not eaten in months.

"Eat quickly you three, it seems that things are getting started down there. Once I get a good idea of what is going on, I will tell everyone what we are going to do." Kravin stood in the same place, never turning around, staring at the field before him. Cher couldn't help but look at the man and see him as if he was a pillar of power, never moving and never wavering from his task.

CHAPTER 5

Destriga and Bear had taken a position on the wall above the great gate that led to the city. The four-story walls that had been built around the city seemed impregnable, yet here was a horde that threatened that belief. It also gave the two commanders the best possible advantage point when it came to surveying the field of battle. The two men stood staring at the field, looking at the horde that was pressing down on the walls of the great city. Both of them exhausted and seeming as if they had not slept or eaten in weeks.

"Well, Des, got any grand ideas on how we should handle this particular situation? Our men are exhausted. We are exhausted and seem to be unable to recover our strength to fight the battle for our men, and to top it all off, we have no reinforcements to speak of." Bear smirked as he mentioned reinforcements, knowing in his mind that without them, their city was doomed to fall.

Destriga turned and looked at the people who moved in the city behind them; he allowed himself a moment of hope as he looked at the people who, knowing what was going on the other side of these great walls, did all they could to live their lives as normal as possible. "Well, I have an idea, which to be honest I think is our best possible plan. Also, I would just like to point out that whether we have reinforcements or not, these people believe in us, which means we cannot allow the Oritha to take this city."

Bear smiled as he looked at Destriga, his booming laugh loud enough to stop the people in the city in their tracks so they could look at their great commander. "Well, you have me interested and ramped up, Des, so let's hear your plan." Bear moved closer to Destriga so the man would not have to talk too loudly. The one thing the two had learned over the years was that it was sometimes best if the men who fought under them did not know what the full plan was, so they did their best to make sure of that one fact.

The two men go back and forth for several minutes before they start yelling orders to their subordinates. Each man who heard his order quickly moved off to whatever position he was told to take. Within a few minutes of the orders being given, the mass of soldiers just outside the city walls began to move and change from men sitting around fires to soldiers standing at the ready. The two men watched as there great battle plan took formation in front of them, adjusting as they saw how the men reacted to their positions.

"Look, Des, I realize we have no guarantee that we will get the help we asked for, but we need to have something ready in case he does show." Bear stood looking like a hardened stone as he pointed to an area in front of the gate. "If we give ourselves some room in the center line here, we can clear out all our soldiers so he can do his thing without any of our men getting hurt."

"Yeah, you're right, but if he doesn't show, then we are leaving our lines at a disadvantage and creating a weak spot that leads right to our front door." Destriga drew a line in the air following the path that their enemy could take through their lines.

"OK, how about we make a deal then." Bear went into describing how he wanted to reduce the number of soldiers in the middle, giving their front line ample room to move through into the city, his gestures getting more forceful as he and Destriga went back and forth about the advantages and disadvantages of planning for help that may not come. Finally, they agree on allowing a small path just large enough for two men to walk shoulder to shoulder through.

The minutes passed as if days as the two men and their soldiers wait for what was sure to come. The Oritha would be upon them soon again this day, and the two men knew that this day would be one of the biggest and most important battles they have fought so far. If their men could just hold out a little longer, they were sure that they would be able to protect their city.

Yet with all their planning, there was one major thing that truly bothered the two men. It wasn't how horrific the fight was that had been going on for so long or how the Oritha had somehow banded together to attack their city. No, it was the fact that somehow, something out there had managed to keep them from regaining their strength. Something they did not know had managed to keep them from having the power to protect their city without calling their soldiers into play.

It was this one thing that ate at both men noon and night. For fifty years these two men had stood as pillars of power within this city and allowed no one to attack it or threaten the people within as they were now threatened. For fifty years, these two men were the only soldiers the city needed. Now, though, the two men looked feeble and unable to even swing a sword if it came down to it.

That was why they had to turn to the man they had faith in. To Kravin, the one man who had been by their side when they started the city. The two had known Kravin for longer than they could even remember now. He had been their best friend before the flare and even more then that after. He had shown them how to deal with the various feelings they had to deal with being as they were now. Watching the people around them grow old and die was one of the hardest things the two men had to deal with, yet Kravin was capable of doing it.

At first they thought him to be coldhearted that not only had he gained great power but also had lost his emotions in the process, but in reality, they had found this to not be true. No, instead this man had become even more caring and even more emotional than ever before. His loyalty to those he loved and cared for not only belonged to those who had died but to those who survived them. That was what he had taught them, the one major fact that they all had to face.

If you truly care about those who had passed, then show their sons and daughters the same caring and compassion you had shown their parents before them. He had taught them not just to care and love those individuals but to care and love their families as well. This was what he practiced and had shown them how to do. It was this one fact that had kept them all sane over the past years. It was also the biggest reason they had created the city in the first place and why they stood doing all they could to protect it.

Both men stood atop the wall above the gate to this great city, both of them seemed to have the same thought at this moment as well. They remembered the day the idea of creating this city had come to them. Though it wasn't completely their idea really, it was actually Kravin again who had shown them how to live in this world with the powers they had gained. Their group at the time had been sitting around the fire; as usual they laughed and drank, enjoying the endless life they had all been given. They had no worries at the time and the only thing that really mattered to them was how they were going to spend their days.

Kravin was no real exception to this either. At times he was the one who enjoyed this more than all of them. It was funny how as they both thought about it, it wasn't the power that had given Kravin such joy but the fact that his friends were with him. His wife was his truest joy, and he at times had expressed the shame and guilt knowing that the women he loved would be by his side for as long as he was alive, whereas for Destriga and Bear, they could not say the same. Their wives had not gained the powers the rest of them had, but it didn't change much, at least not at that time.

Destriga was the one who realized something else at this time though. As he thought about how Kravin had talked about his wife being just as close to immortal as the rest of them yet Destriga and Bears wives were not. It was funny really, they had so much fun at that time, yet Kravin always seemed to have moments where he could not feel joy. None of them ever really thought much about it; none of them really knew how to deal with it or how he could possibly feel so horrible knowing how much power he had.

It wasn't until this day when Destriga and Bear stood on top of the walls of the Garden of Lost Souls that Destriga finally realized what it was that kept Kravin from fully enjoying all the happiness they had all enjoyed shortly after the flare and gaining their power. Destriga allowed a single tear to stream down his cheek as he thought about this one truth. Kravin was not angry with anyone, nor was he truly sad in those moments when he seemed to be lost in some great sorrow. The truth was that he had already thought about the fact that his closest friends were going to lose the most important people in their lives some day and he had no idea how to deal with that.

It seemed he had already been thinking about the future before the past had even settled. Destriga couldn't help but thank him under his breath for caring so much about his two friends. "Say, Bear, you ever thought about how things were before we started the city? How Kravin would party harder than all of us sometimes yet sometimes it was like he was just miserable?" Destriga looked at Bear, not worried about the single tear that clung to his jaw line with all its might.

"Huh, all this time you never really thought about, I take it? Why he was miserable like that sometimes? To be honest, I never really would have thought about it myself had I not overheard the two of them talking one night. I never really thought I would ever see that man cry—I mean you've known him just as long as I have and I am not sure if you ever thought about seeing him cry, but I have since he has seen me cry before. That night though, I swear to you, Des, he cried like a baby in her arms. He constantly kept repeating to her one question over and over again. 'How do I help them? How do I help them when their loved ones are gone?'"

Destriga looked at Bear for what seemed a minute before he finally responded to the man. "Huh, it wasn't something I had really ever thought about, no. I mean as long as we have known him, he has been like that, right? He would just go off into his own world and thoughts, and it always seemed like he was brooding about something. It does, however, give you a good idea as to what he really thinks about. I wonder if that was the type of things he was always thinking about even before the flare."

"Nothing against the guy, but I know for a fact that wasn't the type of thing he was thinking about. Well, at least not all the time. I am pretty sure a lot of the time he was simply thinking about how much he hated who he was. Most of the time when we were sitting around the fire, he was complaining about how he didn't make enough money or how he was single." Bear turned his gaze from Destriga to the battlefield in front of them. "Well, right now it would seem as though we don't really have time to discuss it anymore anyway. The Oritha are making their move." Bear pointed out in the distance as a large mass of dark figures moved across the field towards the city.

Both men stared intently at the mass, analyzing it, trying to see what their movements indicated. They looked at the mass with wisdom and experience from previous battles they had fought before. Though this time, as it was the last week, the two men couldn't base their strategy around what they could do but instead on what their men were capable of doing. They watched as the mass moved forward and began to spread out across the field like a flood.

It took the Oritha only a minute or two to cross the field. In that minute, it was amazing how the emotions that ran through the soldiers outside the city changed like the tides. Fear seemed to hang in the air and overwhelm the ranks of the men as they watched their foe creep ever closer. They fidgeted and rocked on their feet, waiting for what could be their end; thoughts of their loved ones and fear of what would happen after they had been killed paralyzed them all at moments. It wasn't until the commanding officers started barking orders once again at them that the mood changed. The fear fell from the air like a rock and was replaced with zeal, with courage.

In the seconds before the two forces clashed, the men began to yell. Even the two great commanders who stood atop the wall screamed with all their might. Courage was the greatest weapon the people of the Garden had this day. This weapon was the only thing they had that could hold off the Oritha long enough for the reinforcements the two men hoped would arrive.

CHAPTER 6

"Looks like it starting, huh?" Dawg leaned against a tree just to the side of Kravin. He never really looked at the field, yet he could tell that something was taking place. Kravin never really moved at all, nor did his gaze move from the field. A smile crossed his lips as he heard the men from the city begin to yell. It quickly faded as he caught sight of the two men he called his friends. He could see his two friends standing on the wall of the city just above the gate. He could also see that something was very different about the two men.

He looked closely at the two men, using his power to get a better look. It was very obvious to him that something was very wrong. Neither of the men had the auras they once did. Auras that suggested power that rivaled his own, yet now it was almost as if they were normal men. They looked feeble, like their life had been drained away from them. It was no wonder that he had been asked to come and help the city. There was no way that either of these two men would have the strength to do anything if it came down to it.

"You see them too, huh, bro? They don't really look all that well, and to be honest, something smells funny in the air here too. It doesn't seem to be affecting us at all, but something is definitely affecting them though." Still, Dawg never moved his gaze from the soil beneath his feet. It was very obvious though that there was concern in the quiet man's voice.

Cher didn't really know the two men all that well. She had spent time with them after the flare, but she was a friend to Kravin, not much to those two or the rest of the group. Though she had heard a lot of good things about them from Kravin and he did always encourage her to get to know everyone a little better. It was almost like Kravin had this goal of making them one large family, even if they weren't really related. Yet even knowing all that, she felt worried about the two men. It seemed to her as if Kravin may have actually achieved his goal of making them some kind of a family.

"We are going to wait a few minutes into the battle before we make a move. JP, Skinny, be ready to move as soon as I say, got it?" Kravin glared at the battle, and his tone was as firm as usual. As much as Kravin cared about the people around him, it was amazing to those around him how he could shut off those emotions when it came to situations like these. His concentration was unbreakable, and his commitment would never waiver.

They all stood on the cliff as the battle started; the crash of steel and the scraping of claws blanketed the field. The death screams of both men of the Garden and Oritha were like a chorus line of some horrid song. It was the eastern lines that encountered the Oritha first. Like a great wave, they crashed against the steel of the city's soldiers. At first it seemed as though the lines of the city would break, but instead, like a great rubber band, they snapped back into place, pushing the Oritha back.

The line reformed and held the Oritha at bay. Kravin was actually impressed by the strategy his two friends had come up with. The line didn't just push the Oritha back, but it also managed to breathe almost. The men at the front would do all they could to push the Oritha back if just a few feet. Then they would fall back and move behind the men who came up behind them to retake the line. It was a good strategy for the kind of battle they were trying to fight. The idea was not to push back their opponent but simply outlast them.

They could keep their men from getting too exhausted by doing these quick short burst of strength. It wouldn't take too much out of their men, at least not at first. Kravin knew the same as Destriga and Bear that it was the best idea they could come up with at this point. True, they could easily try and push back the Oritha as far as they could, but then a larger problem would occur.

The Oritha outnumbered them, and with that one simple advantage, pushing out away from the walls would be a huge mistake. Once the men had gone so far, they would be spread thin, and there wouldn't be enough men to cover the rear of those who pushed the Oritha back. It would be at this point that all those who had fought to push the Oritha back would give up their lives for nothing. It would be at this point that the numbers would truly count for everything; the garden soldiers would be overrun and destroyed. No, the way Destriga and Bear had decided to do things was the best possible way to do things. By keeping their forces close to the walls, it would allow for their archers atop the walls to help their foot soldiers in the best possible way.

Though Kravin stood here now looking across the battlefield, he could not help but allow his mind to wander just a bit. Looking at those grand walls of the city, he couldn't help but think about the person who lived beyond those walls. He didn't know what she was doing at this moment or how she was feeling knowing that things outside the walls were so bad. Had his friends told her what their plan was, had they even incorporated her in their plans for the survival of this city?

Those thoughts, however, only held his attention for a moment before he began to reminisce about their past and how things had happened between them. It was she who had given him the greatest joy in his life for so many years. It was also she who had caused him the greatest amount of pain in his life. He would never have imagined that things would have turned out as they had, or that their futures would have come together as they did.

To him, she was the single most beautiful woman he had ever seen; of course this may have also been due to the love he felt for her. At first, things between them were nothing more than simple friendship until he developed feelings for her that, at the time, he felt he should not have. He was pretty sure that she did not feel the same way, given the fact that she simply enjoyed his company as a friend and nothing more.

This was the cause of his pain though; he knew that his feelings were not the kind that he should have felt in such a short amount of time, but it seemed as though it was something he was prone to do over his life. The more time he spent with her, the more he loved her, the way she walked or the way she laughed. He remembers vividly the day they had an argument and how he could barely say anything because he was stunned by her eyes.

How with just a bit of makeup—eyeliner, he thinks is what it was called—had made her eyes look like dark emeralds. It wasn't just that though; the expression on her face was something her could not forget. Her brow down and the fury in her eyes at what he had said to her—all of it together painted a picture that he felt was second to none. Yet with all that and everything that had happened between them, the two of them had somehow gotten closer to each other. Of course it wasn't right away; it took some time before anything really happened, and it was something he was not even expecting himself.

He knew as was the case with all his friends that she had not changed at all. Not just the physical beauty that she had, but also the beauty of her spirit and her emotions. He thought it was interesting that someone with such determination would ever find a man like him attractive. After a few moments of these thoughts though, it all came back to him, what had happened those years ago. How he had just left the city without saying anything to her, and he could only imagine how she would feel when she realized he was at the city.

He shook his head slightly, trying to remove the thoughts of her from his mind before returning to the task at hand. The entire line of defense for the Garden had now engaged the Oritha in battle and the same strategy was used across the line. The men would push out and be replaced as they fell back. Watching this, Kravin surmised that the soldiers could keep this up for a while, but soon it would take its toll on them; and when it did, the lines would fail and the soldiers would have nothing left they could do.

He did, however, notice something interesting in the center of the line. A small path set between the ranks of soldiers just wide enough for two men to walk down. He smiled as he quickly figured out what this was for; it was very obvious that Destriga and Bear had set this up in case *he* had entered the battle. They knew that with his power, they would need to evacuate the soldiers from the front line as quickly as possible.

"JP, you will be taking the northern front. The Oritha do not seem to have much of a battle plan at this point, and if I didn't know any better, I would say the idea is just to smash into the soldiers as much as possible until the line breaks. So you should be able to handle it, right?" Kravin looked at JP, his eye letting him know that it wasn't really a question at all. In return, JP nodded firmly, grabbing the straps of his shields and pulling them tightly. Kravin, acknowledging this, turns to Ta and gave her a nod.

Instantly, Ta waved a hand in the air, and a portal opens up in front of JP. The sounds of battle could be heard through it, eliminating all questions as to just where this portal would lead him. JP, smiling, leapt into the portal, yelling a single phrase as he entered. "GET SOME!" As he vanished from sight, the others all giggled a bit to themselves before turning to Kravin for his next set of commands.

"Skinny, you're going south. Same thing goes for you, and for god's sake, try not to kill any of the soldiers, OK." Kravin looked at the man with a judging look on his face. Skinny knew as was the case for JP that this was not a question but a very simple command. In return, he nodded, drawing both glistening swords and waiting for Ta to open a portal for him. This time, Ta did not wait for Kravin to tell her to make the portal but instead opened it right way for Skinny. "GAME ON!" was the cry that left Skinny's lips as he leapt through the portal to the battlefield.

"Well, I assume I will be going to the center line then, brother?" Cher's hands twisted on the shaft of her halberd as she asked Kravin what position she would be taking. Though she was shocked when instead of confirming her suspicion Kravin instead shook his head in disagreement.

"No, sis, instead we are going to the wall with Des and Bear. JP and Skinny should be able to supply enough support for their ranks to pull back a little and reinforce the center line. Also I am curious as to just how cunning our opponent is, so by doing this, I will be able to tell if they are actually smart or if they are really just Oritha who managed to come up with the same idea at the same time." Kravin hesitated for a second before saying anything else. "Ta, if you would be so kind as to get us to the wall, it would be greatly appreciated."

"Well, not sure why they get to have all the fun, but if I have to." Ta, again pouting, created a portal for the rest of them to travel through. She looked at Kravin almost like a small child begging to play with their toys but got no response from him. Understanding that her childish charm would not be working on him right now. She simply jumped on the back of the large beast, which had yet to leave the side of Kravin.

Cher turned to look at the field of battle one last time, trying to imprint this image in her mind. She knew that once she finally did enter the front lines, she would not be able to see things from this point of view again. Quickly, she took note of certain points on the field: certain rock formations and low areas of the field. She knew that it would be unlikely that she would actually see the front-line fighting, but she did have the feeling that she may end up commanding some of the soldiers on the ground below the walls. Then without any more hesitation, she turned and followed Kravin and the others through the portal that led to the top of the city walls. To the friends they had left so many years ago.

CHAPTER 7

Destriga and Bear weren't startled when the five of them stepped out from thin air atop the wall next to them. Instead they seemed to ignore the presence of all five at first. The men, however, who were standing at or near their commanders, quickly circled the five; swords and spears readied to do battle with them. It was Bear who spoke first to his men. "Stand down, everyone, we asked them to come. So I think it would be only morally correct if we treat them with a bit of respect." Bear turned, looking each of his men in the eye, making sure that they all knew that his orders would be followed no matter what happened.

"So, Kravin, from what I understand, you said you weren't going to help us. Actually, if I remember correctly, the exact words were, 'I am not going to help a city who cannot help itself.' Well, it was something along those lines, was it not?" Destriga looked at Kravin; his eyes were those of a weary old man's though he looked to only be in his early thirties.

"Well, that is a discussion we can have at a later time. I believe that right now we have more pressing matters to attend to, do we not?" Kravin smiled a bit at the small game he and Destriga were having. It had been a long time since the two of them could have such a play of formal words together.

"Well yes, I guess you are right, I would also take it that those two men that seemed to appear in our lines out of nowhere are your friends as well?" Destriga pulled his gaze from Kravin and turned back to the battlefield, his movements were as if he were pulling thousands of pounds with him as he did so.

"Yes, they are with me, so if you would be so kind as to let your men know not to attack them, I would really hate for any of your men to end up dead at the hands of those two." Kravin was actually impressed by the view he had at this point. It had been so many years since the last time he watched anything from this spot. From here, the soldiers and Oritha seemed as if they were chess pieces on a board to him.

Bear gestured at a soldier who was standing not far from them and ordered him to tell all the officers not to attack the two men who had appeared. Though it was pretty obvious that the men were there to help, he still wanted to make sure that there was no confusion as to just whose side they were on. He quickly turned back to the field, wondering if these two men were really good enough to turn the tide of battle for them. "Well, I have to hand it to ya, Kravin, those two seem to be pretty good at what they do, huh?"

"Yeah, they are, Bear. To be honest though, they do not have much of anything special. They are fast and strong, at least compared to a normal human, but that isn't what really sets them apart though. JP there, he is a very mild fellow. He never really gets too loud and never really allows his emotions to get the better of him. Skinny, on the other hand, is pretty much the opposite— hot-headed and brash. Alone, they are pretty good. They both love to fight, and to be honest, mainly with each other I think most of the time." Kravin pointed at each of the men as he spoke about them.

"That, though, is not what really sets them apart from everyone. Nope, it is when they fight together as a team that really makes them formidable. JP and his shields seem to stand a hundred feet tall and a hundred feet wide whereas Skinny is like a sniper's arrow. JP can create openings that Skinny is very good at utilizing to his advantage. Hell, they even give Cher a run for her money most occasions." Bear and Destriga both turned to look behind them for the first time, realizing just who it was that had come with Kravin.

A smile crossed the face of both men as they finally turned and saw them. Cher was always a sight of beauty to not only these two men but also to all the men who could see her. Her dark blonde hair, ample chest, and thin waist are every man's dream—although it wasn't just these that made her so appealing to the men around her; it was the way she walked and presented herself that really made her attractive. Her confidence and motherly tone she would take with others too. She did her best at every moment of the day, and her loyalty was never a question. She would never betray those she loved, and she made sure it was well known.

Ta, on the other hand, was almost the opposite of Cher yet just as attractive. Though compared to Kravin, both women were short. Ta, however, was by far shorter then Cher a good five inches at least. Her frame was small and so were her natural assets, yet they seemed larger due to her small frame. Her hair was black like raven feathers, and her smile was always mischievous. Unlike Cher who brought confidence with her stride, Ta brought playfulness and fun with hers. To look into her eyes was to look into the eyes of someone who truly lived for nothing other than simple enjoyment.

Beyond the two women was Kravin's blood brother Dawg. It was funny really sometimes how different they were not just in personality but also in build. Kravin was tall and thin; he had always been like this. Dawg on the other was different; he was short, standing not taller than any average male. His build was different though; his muscles, though not as toned as Kravin's, were larger. Bear knew that this wasn't something that was really natural though. Kravin had always looked toned, but Dawg did not. No, all this mass of muscle he now carried was due to the flare and the powers it had given them. He also figured that Dawg probably trained in order to compete with his brother as the two had done since they were children.

It was interesting really to both Bear and Destriga how these three had clung to Kravin as they did. Each of them were more than capable of doing things on their own, yet Kravin seemed to be the sun and each of them were a planet that was part of the solar system that orbited around him. Anyone who looked at them from outside of this circle would definitely think that this was the case, yet these two men knew better.

They both knew that it was more for the sake of Kravin that these people stayed with him than it was for the sake of them. For all his wisdom and power, Kravin himself was actually weak. Destriga was the one who had started the conversation so long ago that led both Bear and Destriga to the realization of just how important these people were to Kravin. Bear could not really remember what exactly was said that night around the table, but the one thing he did remember was that Kravin had told them both that he drew his strength from the people around him.

Not in a literal sense of the statement but metaphorically. Which in turn was very interesting in itself since his power was very similar to that very statement. Kravin had told them that because he didn't worry as much about his own safety or future, he needed to have someone there with him in order to focus on what he needed to do. It was those people around him that he cared so much for that he really needed to thrive and be the man he once was. Yet at the same time it seemed as though these people also became his greatest weakness. It was his love and care for those around him that made him leave and abandon those who did not want to leave the Garden.

Bear looked at Kravin for the first time since he had arrived atop the wall of the Garden. Almost like the thoughts he had in his mind demanded that he did so. At first, Kravin seemed to have not changed at all since he had left the city, but in reality, he was quite different. He no longer wore the uniform he once did; instead it was almost like a suit from before the time of the flare. Tailored to be slightly larger than he really needed yet it fit him well. The suit blended with his demeanor seamlessly.

It was very obvious that the suit was very old and slightly ragged; strings hung from the cuff and hem of the jacket. Every piece of the suit was faded and no longer held what was probably a once-vibrant color. What was once black now seemed a dark gray; his shirt no longer held the red but in turn was almost a dingy pink. A hole in the left knee of his pants allowed a glimpse of the pale flesh that covered his knee.

All this though was not what really drew the attention of Bear; no, it was the look of the man's face that held his gaze the longest. His sharp jaw line seemed to be even more pronounced than it had been. His eyes, sunken deep into their sockets seemed to glisten in the shadows that covered them. His hair too had changed color somehow, which Bear noted as very odd, considering in all the years that they had lived, none of them had changed in appearance as much as Kravin.

His hair now was a very dark gray, in contrast to the once-vibrant silver it had been when he lived in the city. It was a bit longer as well and disheveled; his brow that once stayed sharp and intimidating now seemed to hang low. He no longer carried himself with the pride he once had, but instead he had a slight slouch to him as if some weight was on him at all times.

The only thing that Bear could really take from what he was seeing at this moment was that somehow, Kravin's powers linked both his physical appearance and his mental state. If this was the case, then perhaps the years he had spent living in the marshes had truly taken its toll on him. It did not really matter though; Bear and Destriga had both discussed what would happen if Kravin had returned to help them. They had both come to the conclusion that they would do everything they could to try and keep their friend from leaving the city once again. Though they also both agreed that they would not use her to try and do so.

"Well, it looks as though things might actually be getting interesting around here, and I don't mean the battle." Destriga had just turned back around from looking behind them within the city. As he did, he thought to himself that this was the one thing that he and Bear both had hoped would not happen. Ironically, within a few minutes of him appearing here, so did she. Perhaps they did have some kind of grand connection that linked them together.

"Shit" was all Bear could mumble to himself when he saw her coming up the stairs to their position. *How could she have known to come here at this particular time? No one had told her we had even notified Kravin of the situation.* Bear combed through his thoughts to try and figure out how this information could have gotten to her so quickly. The only thing he could possibly think of was that it was a mere coincidence. Yet over the years of his life, he knew that one thing was true and that was there were no such things as coincidences.

"Well, I see you came back at a very convenient time, didn't you?" Her voice was soft and low yet carried a sharp point as she addressed Kravin. In return, Kravin did little to even acknowledge her presence. Simply humping his shoulders ever so slightly as if to say it wasn't a big deal. She too never really looked at Kravin but looked at the people who stood around him and the others.

"Cher, you look just as beautiful as you did before. Of course it would seem you have gained a few new scars." The woman looked Cher up and down, her stern face now gleaming with delight. She moved forward before Cher could respond and embraced the woman with warmth. "When was the last time you cut your hair? It has to be a pain trying to take care of it?" The woman took the end of Cher's hair, as if judging how much should be cut off.

"Yeah, I haven't really been worried too much about my hair. I have been training those two idiots for the past few years, which is also where I managed to get the extra scars. I know you're not all that big on it, but if you get a chance while we are here, maybe you can chop some of it off for me." Cher understood what the woman was doing at this point, which was everything she could to not break down in tears.

"Yeah, let me know if you get time, although that really depends on how things go out there, huh?" The woman points to the field of battle that was before them. She took note at the fact that with the two men that Cher had pointed out, the Oritha were starting to lose ground. "I guess you are just as good as you always were, huh? Those two seem to be able to handle this all by themselves?"

"Yeah, they may not be the smartest two in the world, but they are good at fighting, plus they have been itching for a good fight for a long time. Hell, they were so wired a few months ago they even tried to goad Kra—" Cher quickly stopped talking as the woman eyed her. Her glare made it very clear she did not want to hear the man's name at this point.

The beast, Lady as she was called, that had been at the side of Kravin moved quickly when the woman had started to walk closer to the group. It ran full speed at the woman but stopped just short and stared at her. Its mouth hung open, almost in a grin, its eyes fixed on the woman that stood before it. The woman simply reached out her hand and began to scratch the large beast on the head. In turn, Lady moved close to the woman, almost knocking her down, and began to lick the woman's hands. "I missed you too, Lady." Again, her voice was sweet and caring as she comforted the large beast.

"So, Dawg, how have you been?" The woman stood next to Dawg, looking at him. Her eyes were slightly different though when looking at him. It was very clear that she was not really asking Dawg about how he had been but, in truth, was asking how Kravin had been doing outside the city. She quickly turned to look directly at the man when he did not respond right away.

"Oh, um, good been doing good actually. Staying out of trouble and just meddling around the fortress. Doing whatever I can to keep busy and my mind from wandering too far." Dawg could not help but feel nervous around this woman. For some odd reason, it seemed that she could bring any man to his knees simply by looking at him.

"Well, that's good, I am glad to hear that you have all been doing well." The woman stepped toward Dawg and embraced him with even more warmth than Cher. It was as if she was trying to apologize for her forceful question and that she really was glad to hear that he was not encountering any problems outside the city.

CHAPTER 8

The woman stepped back away from Dawg after giving him a hug and turned to walk away from the group. She stopped only for a moment to make one last comment. "Well, I would say it's pretty obvious we have something to talk about at some point. So unless you plan on running away in the night again, feel free to come and talk to me. I am sure you haven't forgotten where I live, right?" Her posture made it very clear that her anger was at a boiling point and that she needed to leave before she became more than any of them could handle.

Kravin didn't turn or even move at this point; closing his eyes, he responded feebly to the woman's request. "Yes, I remember, and if I get time, I will stop by." His face was void of emotion as he spoke, yet his voice quivered. Those around the two knew what the circumstances were between them. Which is also why none of them had said or done anything to get in the way of what they all felt was needed.

It wasn't until the woman had walked away that a single tear ran down the face of Kravin. The guards around them were all startled when they saw this as well. Not because this great man had been brought to tears by this woman but instead by the fact that the tear was not like the tears of normal people. The crimson red that streaked down his face was in fact blood.

"Well, I think that went a little better than expected, wouldn't you say?" Bear quickly spoke up, trying to divert the attention of everyone who was standing around them. He looked at Destriga but could also see the face of Kravin and noticed that the tear that ran down Kravin's face now seemed to be absorbed back into the very flesh of the man. For all the years he had known this man, he still could not get over how disturbing it was to watch this part of the man's powers work.

"Yep, I would have to say that went pretty well actually." Destriga chuckled slightly as he agreed with Bear. His smile was not as convincing as he wished it to be. He also looked at Bear at this time, but it was more like both men were looking at Kravin to see just how he was going to deal with the events that had just taken place. Both men were relieved to see as the tear disappeared and Kravin opened his eyes.

It seemed that after this brief encounter, Kravin had somehow gained a little bit of what he had been missing. He stood a little taller and a little prouder than he had when he first arrived. It was as if speaking to this woman had given him something to think about and fight for. Or on the other hand, perhaps it gave him even more reason to settle this battle as quickly as possible so that he could escape without having to speak with the woman who had some animosity toward him.

"OK, enough of the meet and greet, guys, we need to stick to business here. JP and Skinny can handle a large number of the Oritha on the north and south ends of field. So pull back some of those men and fill in the gap you have in the center line. Which by the way I'm not sure why you two decided that would be a great plan, but I would suggest that you not do that again." Kravin moved his hand in the various directions he wanted the men on the battlefield to move.

Instantly, Destriga and Bear began to call over the various soldiers they had in place to carry messages to the field of battle. From this point, the three men watched as the formations of men began to move and churn, like a piece of clay being molded by a sculptor's hands. Shouts and cries from the various ranks of soldiers filled the air. Slowly over the period of a few minutes, the soldiers that once clustered on the north and south ends of field funneled to the center.

JP and Skinny, who once had to bob and weave around the soldiers of the Garden, now seemed to be even more energetic. They moved through the lines of Oritha like guillotines, hacking pieces from the core of the Oritha ranks. Each time these small pieces would be overwhelmed with soldiers, and nothing could be heard but the wailing of the creatures as they died.

"Cher, go to the center line and make sure those idiots down there aren't doing anything stupid. Oh, Destriga, Bear, could you guys send someone with her to make sure they do what they are told?" Kravin turned quickly from Cher to the two commanders that stood beside him.

"Will do." Destriga gestured to a man as he responded. "Cher, go with this man. He will let the officers down there know that you are going to be in charge. Although I really doubt you would need him to tell anyone. From what I remember, if any of them gave you lip, you would just beat them into submission, right?"

Cher smiled at Destriga knowing that his little joke was intended to bring a smile to her face. She turned to the man who was told to escort her to the battle field. "Well? Are we going, or are you waiting to see just how capable I am with this thing?" Cher pointed the end of the halberd at the man's face, encouraging him to start moving. Instantly, the man turned, and the two were off to the front lines.

"Huh, to think that our forces would get so much help from just two of your people is kind of impressive." Bear stood watching the battle that raged in front him; his eyes darted back and forth between the two men who now seemed to make up the entirety of their army. His expression not really matching what he was saying but instead was one of disgust. The thought of how feeble his soldiers really were turned his stomach in knots as he watched.

"Well, to be honest, it isn't like they haven't had more training than any of your men. Those two have been fighting with each other and with Cher for more years than most of your soldiers have been alive, so I wouldn't really think too much of it." Kravin could tell by the tone of Bear that he was not really happy about the outcome of what was happening in front of him.

"Does it really matter though, Bear? It simply means that our men are not trained well enough and it would seem as though we have been relying way too much on our own power to defend the city. This is exactly why we are in the situation that we are in right now, which means it is something we have to take note of and change in the future." Destriga looked at Kravin as if hinting at the fact that he and Bear both wanted him to return to his home in the city.

"Well, it would seem as though you guys need to get some serious training regimens setup for your soldier then. From what I am seeing, your people don't have a chance at being able to protect this city from any type of threat without the two of you being present." Kravin never returned the gaze of his friend as he spoke, allowing the tone of what he was saying provide the necessary message that he is not interested in staying.

All three men stood staring at what was once a losing battle. Now it seemed a glimmer of hope had come to them in the form of Kravin and those that follow him. Even the soldiers who once fought sluggishly, doing all they could just to hold the ground, had changed for the better. The energy from them could be felt even from the top of the great wall that surrounded the city. The yelling and the clanking of steel could be heard as the men moved and prepared for whatever task they were assigned to do.

This was one of the greatest things Destriga and Bear had seen; even Kravin had to take note that this was a grand feeling. This was one of the things he had always dreamed of seeing: the city and its men full of energy as they did what was necessary to protect themselves. Though the smile that now crossed the face of the great man was not all due to the thought and view of what was happening below him. No; on the contrary, it was always due in part by the thought of Cher down there dealing with all the energy.

Kravin knew that once the men saw her, they at first got the wrong idea as to why she was there; but after a few of them are put in the dirt, they would quickly realize that she was on a far greater scale than they could ever hope to achieve. After that, it would be the even harder task of calming the overly zealot soldiers who suddenly thought they were as strong as JP and Skinny. Though it seemed to be a difficult task, Kravin knew that the woman was more than capable of handling the crowd and all the men in it, simply because she has managed to deal with JP and Skinny for as long as she has without killing either of the two.

"So how long do you think those idiotic creatures will continue to throw themselves at your guys until they realize they haven't got a chance?" Bear almost glowed at the sight of the battle. He could not help himself but feel as though the city would never fall to these horrid creatures especially now. His thoughts raised and screamed at the possibility that the Oritha may leave the city entirely and never return.

"Honestly, I doubt it will be much longer. Either way, whether it is now or hours from now, the boys are more than capable of keeping this pace for as long as needed." Kravin's gaze was not fixed so much on the fight in front of them but on the horizon, on the smoke that drifted lazily up from the forests that were just beyond the field.

"I take it you have noticed the same thing I have? The smoke out there on the horizon? If I am correct, which I think you believe the same, there is someone behind this, isn't there?" Destriga, too, stared at the smoke on the horizon. His brain raced with whom or what could possibly be out there and what exactly they we are planning.

"Huh, to be honest with you two, I never even noticed it, and I have been standing here just as long as you, Des." Bear finally looked past the excitement that was taking place right in front of him to see what it was that was on the horizon.

"That is why I sent only JP and Skinny down there." Kravin, like the other two, now stood like a statue looking at the horizon. All three men combed through their knowledge in order to find a rhyme or reason behind the attacks on the city.

"Hmph, I would never have guessed that you of all people would send just enough out there to stop them. The Kravin I knew would have thrown the full force of his power at his opponent in order to discourage them." Destriga looked at Kravin with curiosity now, wondering what exactly had caused his old friend to start thinking in such ways.

"Well, you are right. I would have done something like that, but to be honest, I am very curious as to who is pulling the strings here and just how smart they really are. So far, I see that they are focusing their attack in the areas where you have the most defenses. Which at first it seemed dumb, but then I thought about it for a bit. Turns out it's actually really smart, as long as you have what could be a near limitless supply of soldiers." Kravin smiled a little, giving kudos to the person in charge of the Oritha.

"Yeah, I get it. If you can just keep throwing an endless supply of soldiers at the main force of an enemy, you will be slowly whittling away at the whole army. On the other hand, why the hell would you want to draw a battle out like that? To be honest, they have been doing this for weeks now, and they haven't gotten anywhere with it. Granted they have killed a large chunk of our men, but still it makes no sense." Bear glared at the horizon in hatred, thinking that someone was toying with his city.

"It isn't that, really. What it really seems it that this person has been waiting for something. They could draw out the battle as long as they employed this strategy and have an endless supply of troops. With that, though, what exactly have they been waiting for?" Destriga lowered his head in thought, scratching his arm as he did so.

"Well, there are a few possibilities: They know something we don't, perhaps some kind of phenomenon we know nothing about. Maybe they are trying to decide exactly what it is they want to do with the city once they take it. Another possibility is that they are simply enjoying the show and savoring the terror they are causing. The last thing I have been thinking about, and to be honest, I believe maybe the best possibility is that they were waiting for someone." Kravin raises his left brow looking at the two men as he did so.

"Waiting for someone? Who the . . . wait . . . you mean they were waiting for . . . you?" Bear's eyes were wide in surprise; his jaw fell, astonished that anyone would possibly do all this just to get Kravin.

"Actually, that makes a lot of sense. If you think about it, they managed to shut us down and then they simply drew out the battle for as long as they can, knowing that we would probably turn to Kravin to save the city. It makes me wish we had not sent Juerg and the others off on a mission." Destriga, now wearing a smirk, was glad that he had finally figured out as to why the Oritha had attacked the city in the first place.

CHAPTER 9

JP stepped out from the portal into a crowd of men. He looked quickly around at this surroundings, figuring out in what direction he needed to move and just how far Ta had put him. He smiled as he saw that Ta had been nice enough to put him only ten feet from the actual line of Oritha and soldiers. His mind was clear except for one simple thought: the thought of how those on the other end of Ta's portals always seemed to avoid them even though you could not see them. It didn't matter though, and he shook his head, clearing it of such a useless thought.

It was killing time for him, and nothing would get in his way. JP stood a head taller than most of the men who were in the army of the Garden. Though a few of the men were just as tall or close to him in height, none of them seemed to have the same kind of build he did. He could tell that a lot of these men weren't even real soldiers; the way they wore their armor or held their swords was a dead giveaway. It was obvious now to him as to why they needed the help of Kravin.

Citizen soldiers were nice to a point. Well, as long as you didn't really want them to do anything anyway. They were poorly trained and even poorly equipped to fight even a light skirmish let alone a battle of this scale. JP leaped over a half dozen men who had banded together just in front of him as he moved for the deeper ranks of Oritha. As he landed, he startled a few of the Garden soldiers, knocking them to the ground. Quickly without a word, he simply grabbed the men and stood them up so they may start fighting again, though he made sure to keep a smile on his face the whole time.

Keeping his wits about him and remembering what it was that Cher had told him about this particular fight, he began to fight his way out farther into the Oritha ranks. His shield bobbed and weaved as he spun, crouched jumped, and jabbed at the foul beasts as he began to move forward. His speed and strength gave the Oritha no chance at stopping him. None of them could match his abilities and skills that had been beaten into him by Cher.

The gray blood of Oritha soon coated every inch of JP as he moved farther and farther into the crowd. Until finally, he found the area in which he was seeking. None of the Garden soldiers remained here now; one, because those who had moved out this far were all dead and because the others had been pulled back, allowing him to go all out. He smiled before he began to taunt the Oritha. "Well, come on, ya bunch of bitches!" He whirled around, striking an Oritha across the temple with the edge of his shield.

His yells of enjoyment were chilling to all those who could hear him. His eyes went blank with bloodlust as he moved. It would have been obvious to anyone watching that this man no longer thought of what actions he would take, but in turn, he simply knew one thing. In actuality, it wasn't even his mind that knew it but his body. The one thing was kill, and it seemed it was something this man had been well trained to do.

On the other side of the battlefield, it was Skinny who leapt forward from the portal that Ta had created for him. Contrary to the way in which JP had turned into a ravaging beast, Skinny did not smile or yell as he moved through the crowd. He was large enough to really startle any of the men around him, but because of this he was able to move through the ranks quickly, striking at the Oritha warriors as he moved.

Countless Garden soldiers gasped in surprise as the killing blow from many Oritha had not fallen but instead the beasts simply faltered and slumped after the blade of Skinny had connected with a vital point. His blade was as precise as it was sharp, and it was something Skinny took great pride in.

It wasn't the ability to fight that Cher had taught Skinny over these years but how to control what he was doing when he was fighting. Over and over, the great woman had ground into him that he was too wild when striking. It took her a long time to break the man of making multiple strikes against an enemy that had already died long before he had fallen.

It was this training that made him such a deadly weapon; calm and collected was what she wanted. It was also something he was more than willing to accept as well. Knowing that with these skills, he would be able to enjoy his fights a little more. Instead of going all out trying to end his opponent, he could now play with them, making strikes that would merely cripple instead of kill. In a short time, he had made his way through the crowd of Oritha and Garden soldiers.

Now he knew it was time for him to truly enjoy the battle around him. There was nothing here to hold him back. Instantly, as if flipping a switch, he moved from Oritha to Oritha with startling speed. Light danced across the faces of his enemy as his blade flashed from slice to slice. After moving twenty or so paces, the man stopped driving his blade into the face of an Oritha warrior. As he drew the blade from the now-dead warrior, he grinned as he heard the death groans of the Oritha behind him, how they had not seen or felt the strikes that had been made against them.

Cher reached down to help the man to his feet who had felt it to be a good idea to grab a handful of her buttock. Her glare added to the already hard lesson learned. Quickly, she began to assess the situation she had been placed in charge of. She could not help but shake her head at the sight of such pathetic soldiers. A small laugh escaped her lips as she figured that either JP or Skinny would probably confuse these men with citizen soldiers.

She knew better though; it was actually very obvious to her but to those two who would not look past the basic impressions gained from the way in which these men carried themselves and their equipment. No, these were real soldiers; they were simply exhausted and poorly trained. It was the scars that the men carried and the calluses they carried that gave it away. Many of these men would be considered veterans when compared to the others.

She knew that these men had just regained some of the energy that they had been spending for the last few weeks, but at the same time she had to keep in mind that they were still exhausted and had not been getting the necessary rest they needed to keep up the fight. She could not push these men too hard, but she could not allow them a single inch on her or they would never give her the respect she needed from them in order to help them.

She now turned her thoughts to giving the orders that needed to be given. She began moving through the crowds of men, looking and analyzing equipment. She had to get the best possible idea of what was going on down here so she could speak with Kravin on what was the best course of action. She also took note of how certain men were faring on the field. Who were the heroes and who were the cowards. All this information she needed to get and quickly.

She barked at many of the commanding officers in the crowd, demanding that they meet here near the base of the wall. She gave these men no room to talk as they all began to gather. Taking hold of the conversation very early, she made it clear as to what she wanted and that no one was to question her authority.

"I want a list of all the equipment we have stored in the area. I also want a detailed list of any soldiers who have displayed exemplary abilities and another list of those who have shown themselves to be cowards. I will handle the duties of commanding this raged army for all of you until you can give me the information I want." Instantly, before finishing what she was saying, Cher walked away with one parting phrase. "You have until an hour after the end of this battle, gentlemen."

She knew had she given them any more time, these men would have begun to argue with her orders. She also knew that she could not allow these men to get a good look at her as well. Given her beauty, these men who were supposedly battle hardened would never respect her if they saw just how attractive she was. She screamed at herself for thinking in such a conceited way, but she also knew that this was something that would happen given the situation. Kravin had told her numerous times that if it weren't for how beautiful she was, she would have been considered the greatest warrior in the Garden before they had left.

CHAPTER 10

The battle raged for what seemed only minutes before the Oritha warriors began to withdraw from the field. At first they started to move slowly but quickly realized the mistake of this decision as both JP and Skinny, taking advantage of the moving forces, began to cut even larger numbers off from the main force of the Oritha. It was astonishing to both Destriga and Bear at how these two men, who were in the middle of the fight, could read the movement of the troops around them and make the necessary decisions to completely crush their enemy.

Both men could not help but think to themselves one large question: just what was it that Kravin was training these men for? Ironically, at the very same time that the two men were thinking this question, Kravin turned to both men and smiled. His smile suggested to the two men that he may have a very good idea as to just what the two men were thinking.

"Well, it would seem that our opponent has realized that I am here and that he no longer has enough warriors of his own to compete with the quality of ours." Kravin turned to leave the top of the wall but was stopped by Bear.

"So we beat them away. Have you put any thought into what we are going to do later?" Bear allowed a little bit of emotion to take control in his statement. Though it was written all over the man's face that he held some worries about the current situation, especially after all three of them have realized the real target was not the Garden but in truth was Kravin.

"Well, to be honest with ya, Bear, I hadn't really thought of it, no. I also have a good reason as to why I have not thought about it either. You think I sent Cher down there just to tell your soldiers not to move from that spot? Sorry, guys, but actually she is doing some spying for me as well. I need to know a little bit more about your army before we can start making the necessary preparations for the next battle." Kravin, never allowing the smile to leave his face, pulled gently away from Bear and began to move down the stairwell that led to the top of the wall. The beast Lady was following behind him, the woman Ta riding on top of the beast as if it were a horse.

Kravin lowered his head and began to whisper to Ta as they moved toward the gate leading outside. "Watch them for me, Ta. I need to know exactly what it is that is keeping them from gaining their powers back." His eyes flared with power again as he fought with the rage that had been welling up in him as he watched the battle.

There was no way that anyone could have known that they would ask him for help. It had been fifty or so years since the last time he set foot in this place. To top it off, no one knew where he had gone to either. It was at this moment that he stopped dead in his tracks; the epiphany that just hit him was laughable to say the least.

Someone knew where he had gone, it was pretty obvious. He had not taken the time to think about it at all. It seemed he was going to need to have a talk with his old friends after he finished his discussion with Cher. Someone had figured out where he had gone and was giving the information out. The real question was just who was interested in knowing where he had gone and what exactly did they want with him.

Again, the same thought crept into his head. Something did not make sense. What would they possibly want with him? He had spent so much time away from everything and everyone that there could be no real reason anyone would go to such lengths to try and lure him out. Granted, if they knew the amount of power he had, some people would try to gain control of it. But what would possibly make them think that attacking the Garden would make him want to help them?

Something was going on around him that he could not fully understand, but he also had a very strong feeling that whatever it was, it was not far from his reach and it was most likely staring him in the face. Once he figured it out though, he would have all the information he would need to completely crush the idiot who had provoked him out of his exile.

Cher stood in the middle of a group of men who at this time had started yelling rather loudly. It took only a second before Cher had gotten fed up with such idiotic banter before she brandished her halberd and began to knock those who would not stop yelling off their feet. "Look, you bastards. I don't have any intentions of arguing with any of you. I am more than capable of cutting all of you in half with very little effort. So give me the information and get the hell out of here. Oh, and please and thank you." Cher added a quick little smile at the end for posterity.

"Well, sis, it would seem as though you are making friends as usual." Kravin smiled at the woman as he walked near her. "By the way, meet me near the rose in an hour so we can go over all the information. Right now, I need to go get the boys before they go and kill off all the Oritha." Kravin smiled and patted the woman's head, as if speaking to a child, before he began his walk toward the battlefield.

Cher growled as Kravin walked away, making sure that he could hear her dislike of how he had just treated her. It was one of the few things that could make her explode in seconds almost every time. It was almost appropriate when he would treat Ta like this; given her size compared to him. On the other hand, to treat her like a child was something that could cause most men to lose their masculinity faster than they could apologize.

"Yeah, sure I would be more than happy to meet you by the garden, ya *asshole*!" Cher had to get what payback she could. What caused her to get even more upset then the treatment was that he would only do it when he knew she would not be able to get any type of revenge on him for treating her like a child.

It was these little moments that Kravin took joy in. He knew in his mind that at some point in the near future he was going to have to pay for it, but he did not care. At the same time, he also knew that given the current situation, he had to do what he could to keep himself in the best possible mood he could. There were very few things in this world that would get his blood boiling, and one of which was threatening his family. At this point, he knew that his family was definitely in trouble.

As he passed through the ranks of soldiers, he took note of those who witnessed how quickly he traversed the battlefield. Only those who were truly paying attention to what was going on around them would notice the fact that his steps did not move him a few feet but instead it

was almost as if he was stepping ten or twenty feet. It
was a trick he had developed a long time ago, using his
ability to teleport short distances as he walked. It had
been a long time since he could use this particular illusion,
but he needed to stop the two boys as quickly as possible
without using too much of his own power.

He had no intentions of actually going the entire way
out into the field but instead just far enough to use
another of his lesser powers. As he moved, he also took
note of the skill of the boys, taking a second here or there
to analyze how efficient they had become with their
weapons. He could tell that both boys had made good
use of the training they received from Cher.

JP, who had a lot of trouble with striking at his foes
when he first came to Kravin, now laid waste to the Oritha
with blow after blow. The shields that had been made for
him had become an extension of his own arms. Kravin
could tell that the sharpened edges were being used to
make attacks to the vital areas of the Oritha warriors'
faces and necks. Though Kravin also took note of the
brutality in which JP fought with, he couldn't help but be
awestruck by how quickly the man would go berserk in a
battle when he was so calm normally.

Skinny though was completely different. At first
glance it seemed as though his wild mentality had been
quelled and his movements were not focused on
dispatching his targets. In truth though, Kravin could tell
that only a few of the Oritha struck down by Skinny had

died quickly. The majority of the wounds were to the major arteries of the poor creatures, allowing them a few minutes of life before they would finally bleed out and die.

"I guess you still have a lot of teaching to do, Cher." Kravin spoke his thoughts aloud as he finally came in range to stop the two boys. He watched for a moment, waiting to see if the two boys would stop on their own accord. He frowned slightly as he realized that the two had been caught up in the heat of the battle.

Kravin's eyes flashed with power again as his mind lashed out at the two men. His thoughts rang loudly in their minds. *STOP!* was all that the two boys heard in their minds. Instantly, both boys stopped as they were jerked out of their battle frenzies. Again, Kravin's thought was heard in the mind of both boys. *The fight is over for now, so get back to the city.* This time, his thoughts were not as forceful but instead kind and caring.

The two boys look directly at Kravin; instantly, the two began to run in his direction, realizing just how far they had moved out from the walls of the city. Their faces at first were twisted in fright, both thinking that they had angered Kravin. Smiles appeared on their faces instead as they realize he was just getting their attention. Kravin returned the two boys' smiles then turned and began to walk back toward the walls of the city.

He had only taken a few steps before he finally noticed the gate of the city. Kravin stopped and began to stare at the grand gate of the Garden of Lost Souls. The soldiers and war machines that were positioned just in front slowly faded away as he stood staring at the gate. It had been so long since he had seen this gate and all its glory. He could not believe that he had ever forgotten just how stunning it truly was.

Though the gates were not really made of gold, the metal that had been used to create it had been dyed to look it. Both doors had taken several years to complete, but it was well worth it in his mind. Each door had a series of leaf-covered vines that wove themselves throughout the doors. In the center was a single rose, and across the petals, the depiction of souls could be seen. The souls melded with the petals, each of which were carved with a smile and seemed to gladly embrace the rose as it absorbed them. That was the idea behind the Garden in a way. This city would gladly take in any who felt as if they were a lost soul.

The smile he had grew even bigger as he looked at this grand image and remembered the meaning behind it. It also brought back many memories of this place and the people that resided here. Two of those people stood out among the rest; it was these two who truly made his memories of this place painful. It was also the memory of these two people that brought him out of his trance, causing him to begin his walk once again back to the city.

The Grand Coward

CHAPTER 11

Bear and Destriga both knew what kind of question Kravin would ask them as they gathered in the great room of the castle. They both also knew that Kravin would be just has annoyed at the fact they neither of them really knew what it was that was keeping them from regaining the power. It would also be brought up about how lacking their forces are when it comes to defending the city.

In truth, Kravin had left the city to them to take care of, and it would seem they had not prepared it as well as they had originally thought. Of course they also had never thought it would be possible for anyone to deny them their power. Even Bear, who had no real power he could project; his being more of a physical type power whereas

Destriga on the other hand use his energy in a more outward way.

Both men entered the chamber before Kravin; it was a mutual understanding that they would need to discuss some things prior to him being included in the conversation. They needed to hash out everything that had happened in the past month and get the order of events together. They had been so caught up in trying to defend the city that they had very little time to think about anything else. Now, though, with Kravin and his reinforcements here, they could rest a little easier and gather their thoughts in order to bring their old friend up to speed.

Destriga combed through his thoughts as did Bear for the first few minutes as the two of them sat in the room. It was Destriga though who first realized the biggest problem the two would have when it came to gathering their thoughts. "Well, Bear, it would seem I cannot really remember much of anything the past the last few days. I would assume this may also be the same case with you?"

Bear nodded in agreement, still squinting, trying with all his might to try and remember details from the past month. "This makes no sense, Des. What the hell is happening to us that we can't even remember what happened?" Bear made no attempt at hiding the frustration behind his comment.

"Not sure, but what I can tell you is that we need to figure something out. We also need to analyze the situation and see if it is going to affect Kravin and his people as well. If it does affect them, then we will have to figure something out to end this war as quickly as possible." Destriga smiled slightly for what appeared to be no reason at all.

"Yeah, that is definitely a problem that we have to go over. I realize Kravin is trying his best not to use his power, but if push comes to shove, we may have to try and convince him to do it. No matter what the consequences are. This city means as much to him as it does to us, possibly even more. Not to mention the other reason; he has to try and keep this city safe." Bear mindlessly ran his hands across part of the table that had been burned.

"You and I both know that is going to be a lot harder said than done, Bear." Destriga never really looked up at Bear as he spoke. He simply sat, looking off into space, smiling.

"By the way, what exactly is it that you are smiling about, Des? The whole time we have been in here, you have been sitting there, staring off into space, smiling for some reason." Bear waved his hand in front of Destriga, trying to gain his attention.

"Ah, it's no big deal, Bear, just something I find funny." Destriga laughed a bit as he responded to Bear's question.

"Just something you find funny, huh? Well, can you at least let me in on the joke because I would love to have a laugh right about now?" Bear turned and looked at the wall Destriga had been staring at, hoping to see whatever it was that had been entertaining the man.

"How long do you think it will be before he gets here?" Bear turned back to look at Destriga, giving up on figuring out what it was that had been keeping his friend so amused.

"Well, I would imagine after he speaks with his two men and Cher. He said he needed to get some information before we could really start hashing out a plan. I would guess the first thing he is going to do is see if those two have been affected by the same thing that we are affected by. The other thing would be to speak with Cher and see just what needs to be done with our forces in order to get them ready for the next battle." Destriga allowed the smile to leave his face as he began to assess the situation himself.

Kravin entered the city through the gate he had just been admiring and stopped just inside the city walls. Cher was standing just off to the side of the entrance waiting for him. The look on her face told him that the situation with the soldiers of the city was a little worse than he had originally anticipated. "So, Cher, just how bad is it?"

"Well, for starters, the men are all exhausted. To be honest, I can't believe they have managed to defend the city as long as they have. Add in the fact that their equipment is old and ratty, they have very little training, and they lack the numbers to really defend the city on their own. Simply put, either we are going to be putting in a lot of hours doing this ourselves or this city is going to fall. We do not have the time or the resources to get these soldiers up to par." Her face was filled with both pity and disgust as she spoke.

"Well, I guess we will just have to make do with what we have. Either way, though, see what you can do. Eliminate the soldiers who aren't worth having on the front lines and have them start working on making equipment. Also start training in shifts right away. Those who have the energy need to start now. Let the boys give them the basics and you work on the veterans and officers. *We* need to get these people better situated as soon as possible." Kravin glanced quickly side to side, never really looking at Cher as he spoke.

"All right, I will see what I can do, but I am not making any promises. These men need years of training and you want me to do it in hours. Anyway, how long should I make the shifts? We still need some men on the wall as well." Cher pointed upward, reminding Kravin that the Oritha had only withdrawn for now.

"Lady is still up there, she will let us know if anything starts happening. Besides that, train the men just outside the gate. That way you can keep watch at the same time. As for the length of the shifts, I don't really care. I guess whatever you feel is going to get the best results." Kravin continued to ignore her gaze and looked off into the crowd of people moving around the city.

"OK, oh, and so you can calm down, I heard that she stays near the church most of the time so you won't have to worry too much about running into her." Cher flicked her hair as she walked away from Kravin.

"Thanks" was all Kravin said as he began to move through the crowd toward the large castle that was positioned in the center of the city. It wasn't until after this that he suddenly stopped and smiled. As soon as the smile spread across his face, the man disappeared, startling a few citizens in the process. Instantly, Kravin had been teleported from his post on the road to just outside a large wooden door. On either side was a single torch, behind them streaks of black ran upwards towards the ceiling, showing everyone who passed by that these two torches had been burning here for a long time.

On the other side of the doors, Destriga and Bear were in the midst of a conversation that at this very moment seemed to carry an even larger weight on their future and the future of the city than the one involving the battle raging outside—a conversation about the man they have known for so long and have missed for just as long. They both knew that Kravin possessed the power they needed to defend the city, but they also knew that it wasn't just his power they needed.

"Aside from the common issues relating to the Oritha and the fact that something seems to be keeping us from recovering our strength, we also need to figure out what we are going to do about Kravin. He has a way of looking at things that is different from either one of us. It is this kind of thinking that we really need right now. I mean I can think about things in a strategic point of view and you are pretty good at coming up with things on short notice, but Kravin on the other hand is a problem solver. He always has been. He sees things that we don't and can give information about things we may never even think about. On top of that, to be honest, I miss having him around. I am also sure that there are others here who miss him as well, and for their sake, we need to figure out a way to keep him here." Destriga pointed in a direction as he said the last part of his statement.

"Yeah, it does seem like something has been missing these past years without him hear, Des. You are also right that I am sure they miss him as well. The only problem is we tried to keep him here in the first place, and he didn't listen to us then. What makes you think that in the past fifty years that anything has changed to make him finally start listening to us now?" Bear sat looking at Destriga with a curious look, hoping that his friend had noticed something about Kravin that he himself had missed.

"Well, there is something a little different about him now, but I cannot really put my finger on it. It isn't his attitude or anything about that or how he carries himself. Well, actually I am wrong. That is part of it." Destriga lowered his brow as he began to think about what it was that he noticed about his friend.

"What do you mean there is something different about his attitude?" Bear sat up in his chair, moving closer to the table, eagerly awaiting Destriga's response.

"No, not his attitude, but the way he carries himself. He still walks with the pride he has always walked with, but something is different about it. His steps used to be very crisp and clean, *exact*—for a lack of a better word. Before, it was almost as if every step he took was planned out in every detail. His feet shuffle more, and I noticed that he sometimes drags one of his heels, which if you remember was something he found very annoying. It almost seems as if there is something weighing on him. I am not sure what." Destriga looked at Bear with what appeared to be a worried expression on his face.

"Well, that very well may be true. I realize he has been with Cher, Ta, and Dawg for all these years, and apparently those two boys, but it isn't like he didn't leave anything important behind here either. Aside from us, there were others as well, which you and I both know. Kind of wish we had not sent Juerg and the other out. I bet Juerg would be able to get him to stay or at least annoy him enough to get him to hang out for a bit. Juerg seemed to have some connection with him that you and I did not have." Bear sat back in his chair, staring up at the ceiling of the room. His mind wondered off, thinking about the possibilities of what could have been.

Just as the two men were finishing their conversation, the doors to the room opened in a grand gesture. Both men looked, already knowing who it was that had just entered the room. Kravin stood before the two men in the doorway of the room, one hand on each door and a simple smirk on his face. Both men who had already been in the room cannot help but think of how things had once been when this man spent a lot of his time in this room.

"I take it that was your little woman who was trying to get in here earlier?" Destriga smiled at Kravin as he said this. His smile letting Kravin know that it wasn't really a question as much as it was a statement. It was also a smile of joy seeing his friend in this place once again, and finally after the days of fighting, they had just a few moments to act as if they were the friends they once were.

Kravin laughed at first, a small laugh amused at the fact that Ta had actually tried to follow these two men in to this room. He thought to himself about the irony of that particular fact, simply because Ta had known before that she could not enter this room unless one of them had allowed it and never through any way except these doors. "Well, I guess so, although it is a little funny that she actually tried. We told her countless times before that she wouldn't be able to do it."

"Yeah well, it never hurts to try, right?" Bear stared at his friend, a smile crossing his face as well. His brother had returned to his place at the table this day. Bear made a promise to himself at that very moment that he will not let this man leave this city again.

"So what would you two like to speak about first? At this point, I have spoken to Cher and have gotten a pretty good assessment of what is going on in your army and just what needs to be done." Kravin walked to a chair that was covered in dust and webs. It was obvious that no one had used this chair in a long time. He stopped for a moment, looking at the floor, noticing the various signs of the chairs movements. Signs of what the man who once sat here had done quite a bit.

"OK, well I guess. What exactly do you think is the biggest priority right now?" Destriga no longer wore the smile he had when Kravin entered the room. Instead, his face was one of great concentration. He leaned forward, setting his elbows on the table, giving Kravin his full attention.

"Well, as I said, I have already spoken with Cher. So far between your soldiers' poor skills, they also lack quality equipment, and they are all exhausted. So with that being said, I have already given Cher instructions on how to handle the situation for both. The first thing is to get the men on a training schedule that rotates the men in and out. Cher will be doing the training for your veteran soldiers, and the boys will be giving the novice instructions. I do not want every one of them training at the same time either." Kravin never sat in the chair he had walked to; instead he chose to stand, setting his hands on the table and leaning forward as he talked to Bear and Destriga.

"You said that they are going to be rotating in the training . . . what exactly do you mean by that?" Bear looked at Kravin with a look of confusion, not fully understanding what Kravin is thinking or planning.

"Well, it is pretty simple, Bear. The soldiers will be broken up into the three groups. Each will have a schedule of being on guard training and rest. This way, the men can get constant rest but also get training." Kravin returned the gaze of Bear, looking to make sure his friend comprehends what it was that Kravin was saying.

"Well, that sounds like a good plan, except it doesn't really take care of the problem in a quick manner. I mean if they are rotating in and out of training, guard duty, and rest, then it would mean them learning what they need to know at a slow pace. Which in turn it would seem as though it won't be all that in the short term." Destriga never moved as he spoke. He simply looked at Kravin, hoping that his friend has a good explanation as to why he felt this to be the best course of action.

"Well, you are right. This particular method isn't going to get the men trained at a very high rate of speed. At this point though, the men are so exhausted they wouldn't really learn much from the training at all. Also, they would never be able to handle the full regimen, either which would make the training futile. On the other hand, by doing this, they will get used to this type of life. To be honest, I am not looking at a short-term goal here, gentlemen. I am looking at the long term. My people are more than capable of handling the threat of the Oritha at this point." Kravin stood up, removing his hands from the table. His expression made it clear that he would not allow his plans to be changed by these two men.

"Long-term, huh? So I guess that leads into the question that I believe Bear and I both want to ask. If you are thinking long-term, then would that also mean you are not planning on departing the city anytime soon?" Destriga leaned back in his chair, his eyes showing curiosity and hope.

"I will stay but only for a short term. When I say short, I mean a few months at the most. I also need to figure out what it is that is affecting you two. So I will be sending Ta out to gather some information on that problem. Since it would seem you two do not have that capability at this point. Which leads into my next question, where exactly is Juerg and Angelus?" Kravin raised his right brow as if to say he was expecting a good excuse for their absence.

"Well, we had some issues in the north with some trade routes, so we went ahead and sent them to handle it. We have not yet heard anything on that situation as of yet, but I am sure those two can handle it without a problem." As Bear responded to Kravin's question, his expression changed to one of surprise.

"Well, from the look on your face, Bear, it would seem you just thought of the same thing I did." Kravin smirked at his friend, slightly impressed of his friend's ability to notice the same thing Kravin had.

"What do you mean? What is it that you two just figured out?" Destriga seemed troubled as he realized there was something he had missed in the conversation between Bear and Kravin.

"Des, to be honest I can't believe that you haven't noticed it yourself. The problems with the north trade routes all happened within a week of the first attack on the city. Don't you think that is a little too convenient?" Bear looked at Destriga with anger in his eyes. Not anger at his friend but at himself and their opponent. Anger directed at the fact that they had not noticed this fact a bit earlier.

"So it would seem someone really wanted to get you out of retirement there, brother." Destriga looked at Kravin has he spoke. His eyes reflected that of Bear's and Kravin's. All three men stood around the table, looking at each other. Each one racking his brain trying to figure out who it was that had gone to such lengths to draw Kravin back to this city once again.

CHAPTER 12

It had been a long time since the people of the city had been as relaxed as they were this night. The people had seen the first victory of the war since it had begun. It was all this night that the city would rejoice in this victory and in the hope that had returned to the city. People moved throughout the streets in preparations for a great celebration that would be held in honor of the victory.

Lanterns that were once used only for the most special of occasions had been set up along the city streets. Laughter could be heard from the children as they played, mimicking the actions of the heroes who had participated in the battle. Men spoke in groups as they walked, talking of the war and how the soldiers had all been assigned special training. Discussions of how the various shops producing the equipment for the soldiers were going to begin to thrive as requests poured in for new equipment.

The women of the city packed in clothing shops and traveled through the city in a hurry. Each of them spoke of dresses and of the men they wished to attend the festivities with. Some spoke of their husbands and how proud they were of how they were handling things in the city. Others spoke of potential suitors for their daughters and possible wives for their sons.

The city seemed alive once again this day, and it was all thanks to the man Kravin who had once forsaken the city. Yet to all those who walked in the streets or crowded in to shops and tavern, there were two heroes this day, neither of which was Kravin. No. Instead the two men who were deemed the heroes of the day were JP and Skinny.

The two walked through the crowds of the city boisterous and full of ego of the fame that had been given to them. Both men flirted with women who caught their eyes and shook the hands of the men who greeted them. They welcomed the fame and glory that had come with the day's battle. Yet with all the glorious treatment and praise neither of the men forgot who the real hero was this day.

They both knew that Kravin was the single hero this day. Had he not made the choice to come to this city, neither of them would have done anything to help. This single thought was the only thing that truly kept the men humble in some way. Though they were gifted with great physical powers and a link that none of them could explain, neither of them could compare to the power that Kravin fought with and kept in check every minute of the day.

Cher watched as the people of the city prepared for their grand celebration, and though she knew that the battle was not truly over, she also knew that the people of this city were doing the one thing they really needed. For once since the start of the siege, the people of this city could relax and enjoy the time they had together. She also knew that the men she had before her wanted nothing more than to enjoy the festivities that the others would be enjoying this night.

She never allowed her mind to slip though; her attention may become diverted for a second or two here and there, but she would not allow herself to become completely distracted. She constantly was yelling orders at the men she was training, slapping various body parts of the men who seemed to have the most trouble getting what it was that she was telling them to do. Cher knew that in order for these people to have the lives they once had before the siege had started, she would need to train these men as hard as possible without breaking their spirit.

It was when this thought entered her mind that the woman she once called sister appeared in the area in which Cher trained the soldiers. Her expression was one of concern and care for the men who stood before her. "Cher, do you really think it is a good idea to keep these men from their families tonight?" Her voice was low and quiet, yet it seemed to carry as far as the eye could see.

Cher knew the men she was training could hear her, but they all knew that it would not be in their best interest to stop what she had told them to do. "Actually, that was something I have been going over in my mind, sister. These men need a lot of work before they are capable of defending the city themselves, but I also know that they need a night off." Cher never looked at the woman as she spoke; instead her eyes analyzed the men training before her. Catching a lack in posture in one of the men, Cher did not hesitate to whack the man with the end of her halberd to correct it.

"Well, I can tell you that it would be greatly appreciated by all the wives and mothers in the city if you allowed the men to participate in the celebration tonight. Besides, I know Lady is still on the wall, so it isn't like the city won't be protected." The woman turned as she finished her statement.

"All right, sister, I will give in, but that will mean I will have to cut the rest time of all the men in the next rotation in order to make up for what they have missed." Cher made eye contact with every man that stood before her. Her look was enough to tell the men that they will pay for this time of celebration they had been given. "Also you, will all be under strict rules during the celebration, and if you think I won't know if any of you break the rules, you are sadly mistaken."

All the men at once stopped their training and looked at Cher. Gathering in a line, the men all saluted. "THANK YOU, MA'AM!" was all the men said as they broke their line and again returned to training.

Cher could not help but smile at the results she had just seen from the men's training. She had never expected the men to have such respect for her given the cruel treatment she had been giving them in their training. Though she also realized that these men must have a great understanding of the situation their city was in. She praises these men in her mind as she again corrected a man's posture with the blunt end of her halberd.

She turned to look for the woman who she had just spoken with. She was disappointed to find that the woman had merged into the crowd and disappeared. It had been a long time since the two had been able to engage in a conversation. It had brought back memories of a time of joy for her as they spoke. Though she missed these conversations, she also knew that she had more important things to attend to at this particular time. Instead of allowing it to get to her she instead promised herself that the two would have one of these conversations one more time before they departed for the fortress once again.

After having his discussion with Bear and Destriga, Kravin had wandered around the castle for a while. His mind wondered from memory to memory as he moved through the hallways and rooms of the castle. His feet where heavy once again and his once-proud demeanor giving way to the weight he seemed to carry. So many things had happened here throughout the years he had lived here. He also thought of the fact that he never expected to ever return here.

It had been an hour or so after leaving the great room, that he had come to a place that seemed to almost bring the man to his knees. He had not planned on coming to this balcony, yet his feet seemed to have carried him here of their own will. Of all the places he could have wandered to, it was this place that he finally ended up.

"Why of all the places in this castle would I walk here? Granted it is one of the most precious memories I have, but it is also one of the most painful." Kravin spoke his thoughts aloud as he looked out from the balcony across the great expanse of the city that lay before him. Between the memories of the past and the sight of the celebration that was to come this night the weight seemed to be more than even he could carry.

It was not until Ta appeared on the edge of the balcony that his mind stopped long enough for him to compose himself. Her expression was different for the first time in the last few days. She no longer smiled gleefully at the chaos that was around her but instead looked at Kravin with concern and curiosity. "Ya know, if it hurts that much, why don't you just stay away from places like this?"

"Sorry, Ta, but I wasn't exactly planning on coming here. I actually was just wandering around the castle and ended up here." Kravin smiled lightly at the small woman, patting her on the head. His smile was the only expression of thanks he would allow himself to express to the woman for caring about him.

"Well, whatever . . . if that's your excuse, then I guess I will have to except that. On the other hand, I I would like to point out what a guy once told me a long time ago. You should never allow the past to control your present or your future." Ta allowed the smile to return to her face as she said this. Her eyes beamed with pride knowing that she was throwing the words of Kravin back at him in order to snap him out of his sadness.

"OK, I get it, Ta. By the way, did you forget that you wouldn't be able to port into the room, or did you just not care?" Kravin finally looked away from the view of the city as he asked this question to Ta.

"Na, I didn't forget, but I still never got the chance to actually test it. Besides, now we know that no one can." Her smile had dawned on her face once again, knowing that she was saying things to Kravin that he himself would say.

CHAPTER 13

The people of the Garden had spent the entire afternoon planning for the celebration, and they were finally ready—ready to enjoy the evening and, for just a few hours, forget all about the enemy that waited outside the walls of the city. The men and women had all gathered the food and beverages that would be served, and now they were putting on their celebration attire and making their final arrangements. Wives and husbands could be heard urging their children to hurry and get ready.

The young men of the city were all eager to see the various beauties that they all had their eyes on. In turn, the young women also had high hopes in seeing the men that would be at the great hall. Slowly at first, they all began to gather at the hall that was positioned just outside the castle. Many of the people at this time were under the impression that the great castle that watched over the city was the center. The truth though was different because Kravin had been the man behind the layout of the city.

It was his desire to put this grand hall at the center and the castle just behind it. Though the castle was an important part of the city, it was the hall that Kravin had chosen to be the center. It was here that he wanted the people to gather and enjoy the lives they were given. It was the one place where the people could come and forget the burdens of their daily lives. So he a dubbed the great hall the Heart.

The name was simple, but it was also the only way to describe the way Kravin felt about the hall and what it was for. It was here that the people of the city would gather to see the marriages of the young. Though it was not all about enjoyment; funerals were held here as well. In reality, this one place was welcome to all matters of ceremony. Because of this, it was truly the heart of the city.

Tonight though there would be no weddings or funerals. No births to be celebrated; no, tonight was celebration of the city itself. A celebration of hope, hope for the future of the city and the people that lived in it. It would give thanks to those who protected the city. Not JP and Skinny but all the men and women who fought just outside the walls to keep the city safe. Tonight there would be many celebrities here all of whom carry a sword and a shield.

As was the custom, Bear and Destriga were the first to arrive at the hall. In the past, when Kravin and the others were still at the city, they would all be the first to gather at the hall. Each of them taking a seat at the long table that stretched across the far wall. Tonight, though, only two men sat at the table waiting. They sat in two of the high-backed chairs that had been carved for them.

The chairs were aged; crafted long ago by steady hands for the men who ran this city and protected it. Though the high-backed chairs seemed to be the focal point of the table, they were not the only ones. One chair was placed in between Destriga and Bear, it too being a high-backed chair and just as intricately carved as the other two. On the other side of both Bear and Destriga were placed four chairs. Each of which was meant for one of the people who were considered to be the leaders of this city.

As the people entered and saw that only two of the eleven chairs were filled this night, it was as if the energy of the people slowly faded. Adding to their woes at the lack of leaders in the city at this time of need, they also saw that the two men who were sitting at the table were fatigued. They could not help but seem desperate seeing that the two great men who were thought to be immortal looked half dead sitting behind the great table.

Neither Bear nor Destriga allowed their smiles to waiver, though. Both of these men knew that they needed to inspire their people as much as they could. At this point, given their fatigue, they could not do battle and inspire them, so instead they kept their smiles bright. They each greeted the people as they entered, making sure to use as much energy as they could. Slowly the number of people who entered the hall began to quicken.

Within a half hour's time, the hall that once was empty was now packed. All the people who entered all sat or stood; their attention was upon the table. It was focused on the two men who sat there; they all waited with anticipation as to what these two men would say. The energy that had slowly started leaving the people now gathered again. *What would Bear and Destriga say and who were the men who had saved the city?* Were the thoughts of all the men and women in the hall.

Destriga was the first to speak of the two men. Slowly he stood and looked out at the crowd of people before him. Returning a few waves from various people in the crowd, he cleared his throat. "If you have come to hear information on what is happening outside the walls of this great city, I am sorry to disappoint you, but I will not be speaking about that. No, that is not what this celebration is about tonight."

Bear at this point stood next to his friend, and he too began to speak to the people who have gathered before them. "People of the Garden, we are here as family. We stand and sit here next to those whom we care about and those we see every day. We have gathered here from all walks of life, rich and poor. We are here to celebrate this great city, not a great battle. "

Destriga again began to speak, timing his comments to follow as soon as Bear finished his sentence. "We all have lost loved ones in the past weeks of battle. Tonight, we celebrate them as well. Our families are not destroyed. We may have lost many of us these past weeks, but that does not mean we are not going to carry on."

"Keep in your hearts this one single thought. In this city, we are not simply people with nowhere else to go or no other way to live. No, in this city, we are all family, and when one of us loses a loved one, we all lose a loved one. Tonight, we are family as we are every day, and our family is whole. So tonight, we gather as a family and celebrate each other." Bear raised his mug in the air as he spoke these final words.

Destriga too raised his mug and looked out in the crowd. A smile crossed his face as he saw Kravin standing just inside the doors of the hall, his hand held a filled mug. His mug too was raised to in the air, acknowledging the feelings of the two men at the table. Destriga looked at Bear form the corner of his eye and saw a smile too across his face. It was obvious to him that Bear was seeing the same sight as he.

The crowd cheered as they all raised their glasses and mugs, showing that they too agreed with what Bear and Destriga had just said about the city. At once, the entire crowd of people, including Destriga, Bear, and Kravin, drank from their raised glasses. It was at this point that the band began to play. Finally, the celebration had officially begun, and the people of the Garden of Lost Souls could relax.

The beginning of the celebration was full of food, laughter, and conversations. Many of the people approached the table of Destriga and Bear, all of whom desired to know the names of the two men who had been deemed the heroes of the city. Each time they were told that the men were in attendance of the celebration and that they could and ask them.

Soon, the food had all been cleared away. Tables that were once used for eating now were placed off to the side of the room. The people of the city used the now-open area to dance to the harmonies of the band. Men and women of all ages moved across the hall, all of them looking for a suitable dance partner.

Kravin had never moved from the spot he had acquired just inside the door. He simply stood, drinking the mead he had been given. He watched as the people of the city, for the first time since he had returned, relax and enjoy their lives. He could not help but be happy at the sight of this because this was, in truth, the one thing he wanted for all the people of the Garden.

Cher too had decided to attend the celebration; though she did not get to the hall until after the dancing had started. As she entered the hall, she found Kravin in his position just inside the doors. "I find it hard to believe that you would come here. Considering the fact that you are trying to avoid her altogether, being here almost invites an encounter."

"To be honest, I had forgotten all about it. I was more interested in seeing the people of the city enjoy themselves. I wanted to see if they were still capable of living the way I had always wanted them to." Kravin never looked at Cher as he spoke; instead he simply smiled as he watched the people of the Garden dance and converse amongst themselves.

"Well, if that's the case, let's go." Cher grabbed Kravin by the hand, causing him to drop his mug. She did not allow him the time to respond or pull away but instead led him toward the center of the newly formed dance floor. Her smile was wide, catching the eye of many men as she passed by. None of whom stood in her path seeing her pull Kravin through the crowd.

Kravin had not noticed that Cher too had chosen not to wear her armor, but instead a gown like the rest of the women who were at the celebration. He had known her for some time, and he had never denied the fact that she was a very beautiful woman. Tonight, though, he could not help but be mesmerized by her beauty.

It was unlike her to wear gowns or act like a normal woman. No, she had not grown up to be this kind of woman. Instead, her life had made her a self-reliant woman, one who did not worry about how she looked but instead how she would take care of herself. She had been a mother at a young age and had made those children her pride and joy. Kravin had always envied her, envied her determination and will to take care of those children. To him, it was not just that she was physically beautiful, but her personality was second to none.

With all that, he could not help but see the woman that she was tonight. Her hair had been pulled back and done in an ornate ponytail. Her gown hugged her body in all the places needed to turn a man in to a lump jelly before her. To him it was the best thing she could have picked for herself. Her ample chest filled out the gown and provided just enough cleavage. The bottom of the gown slit to the thigh, allowing it to move and give a glimpse of her amazing legs. The back cut down to the middle of her back.

With all her beauty amplified by the gown, Cher could dance with any man she chose tonight. Knowing this, Kravin felt sheepish knowing that his attire in no way complimented the beauty that stood with him on the dance floor. He felt as though he was doing her a dishonor by looking so disheveled. Yet he did not seem to bother her in the slightest. Instead, she simply raised his hand and moved close to him.

"You remember how to do this right?" was all she said as she placed her hand on his shoulder and raised their other hands.

Kravin smirked slightly as he responded, looking around in embarrassment. "Yeah, I think can manage." Kravin placed his hand on Cher's hip, and the two began to dance. They moved slowly, enjoying the time together. Slowly, the noise around them faded, and nothing could be heard by either of them.

Cher cannot help but think about how great the man before her is. Though he may not believe it himself, she felt he was one of the greatest men she has known. It was like a dream to her to be standing in this place dancing with Kravin. Slowly as they danced, she moved closer to him, allowing her hand to fall from his shoulder to his chest. Lightly, she placed her head too on his chest, smiling as she began to hear the heart that beat in his chest.

"Ya, know, Kravin, I have dreamed of doing this on more than one occasion. Being here in the great hall, you holding me in your arms as we dance—it's like I am dreaming. Though I never thought I would be wearing a gown like this, but tonight, I felt like wearing something like this." She moved her head ever slowly, slightly snuggling as close to Kravin as she could.

"Well, I never thought I would see you wearing something like this either. Even so, I would have to say you look rather stunning in it." Kravin could not help but smile as he looked down at the woman in his arms. He had known her for so many years, but never had he seen this side of her. She seemed so fragile in his arms; he could not ignore that this moment was a gift to him from her.

"Thank you, and I am sorry. I know this is something you probably did not want to hear from me. Though it should be pretty obvious how I feel. I just really wanted for once to know the joy that she was given. For once, I didn't want to be looking from the side with jealousy on my mind, but instead I wanted to be the one you held. I know I will never have your heart the way she does, but just this once, I would like to feel like I do." A single tear streaked down Cher's face as she speaks to Kravin.

Hearing the words of this amazing woman pierced the heart of Kravin. He did not respond but instead smiled as he leaned down and kissed the woman on the forehead. His eyes and smile made it very clear to Cher as she looked up at him that he was grateful for the woman's admiration. His eyes though also expressed the anguish he felt for not being able to return Cher's love for him.

As Cher looked into the eyes of Kravin, she knew all too well that she could not have a spot in his heart as big as another's. She could not help but allow a few more tears fall from her eyes as the hope she had faded. The smile never left her face though as she looked at him. She still appreciated the understanding he had for her. She knew that this man wished with all his heart to care about her the way she cared for him. Yet his heart would not allow him to love her as strongly as he loved another.

Cher knew that this moment would end at any second, but she could not help but wish that it would never end. She shook her head slightly, trying to get the dream from her mind. It was not realistic for her to dream of this because she knew that the moment that woman stepped into the hall, she would be the center of Kravin's attention. It was as if she could see the future, for as she thought this very thing, the woman who truly held Kravin's heart stepped into the hall.

Kravin was not looking in the direction of the doors, instead giving his full attention to the amazing woman who was currently in his arms. Something though at that moment pulled his attention from her. No amount of will power could have stopped him from focusing on the beauty that had just entered the hall. For a second, it was like she had been surrounded by light, blinding him and allowing him to only see a shadow.

This blindness lasted for only a second; once it had passed, Kravin could not believe the sight before him.

Unconsciously, he stopped moving with Cher and slowly let go of her. Cher in turn knew that this would be his reaction; though jealous now, she knew there was no way for her to change his reaction. Looking at Kravin one last time, she simply said, "Thank you." She moved from the floor, disappearing into the crowd, her moment of joy now over.

Kravin stood in the middle of the dance floor, his eye fixed on the beauty that had just entered. Not just Kravin though; all but a handful of the men in the hall stared with lust in their eyes. They knew this woman, and they all knew that no man could hold her heart. None who had tried before had been successful. Yet there were a few in the crowd this night who knew the truth.

They knew that this woman had fallen for a single man. Her love was for him and him alone, yet at this moment, it had seemed as though those feelings had faded over the years. Now she seemed as if she had only cared for the others of the city. She spent her days in the church of the city, helping those who were truly in need. Her priority was not in seeking a relationship for herself but instead caring for those around her.

Kravin was one of those who knew the past of this woman. He knew all too well the pain that she had endured because of the love she had. It was this thought that brought the regret and shame flooding back to him. Those memories were like a flood engulfing his mind as he watched her walk toward the dance floor. It was these memories that paralyzed him, keeping him from moving into the crowd and hopefully from her gaze.

It took her only a minute or so to reach the point where Kravin stood. Her eyes were like ice as she looked at him. She never once looked in any direction but his; never did she allow anyone or anything to have her attention but the man who stood in the middle of the dance floor. Her steps were long and graceful, causing the long gown she had donned to flow around her.

Kravin watched as this beauty clad in a snow-white gown walk toward him. It had always been this way though. She had never been the kind of woman to think she was beautiful. In truth, it pained her to wear such things. Yet for all her lack of self-confidence, he could not help but be awed by her breathtaking beauty whenever she would wear such things. She was a tomboy at heart, yet when she did act feminine, it was impossible for the men around her to not be hypnotized by her beauty.

Not even Kravin was immune to her charm, and at this moment, he could not take his eyes from hers. Again, she wore the eyeliner that she once wore, and again he felt as if he would melt before her gaze. Her hair, light in color, had been pulled up, held by an ornate comb. The gown she wore was of the purest white and modest. Yet it still highlighted the curves of her body and amplified them. The lack of sleeves allowed the men to see her toned and sensual arms, lightly tanned by the sun. She wore no other makeup than the eyeliner, and the jewels in her ears were nothing more than simply hoops.

The dress wrapped around her neck, allowing no view of her chest, though it was still hard for any man to not notice the fullness of her bosom. To Kravin, the sight before him was one that was as close to perfection as he had seen in a long time. The only thing that disturbed him and made him eager to move was the look that the woman carried on her face. He knew why she was here and what she had in mind as she walked toward him. He hoped that she would not cause too much a scene when it happened.

"It looks as though you have not run away yet." The woman's voice was soft yet carried a hint of maliciousness in it. Her gaze was full of fire, fire that was hot enough to burn anything that it was set upon.

"My job isn't done yet, Katie, and until it is, I won't be leaving." Kravin stood before Katie with as much ego as he could muster. He would not allow his pride to be hidden, not in front of everyone here. He quickly hid his hands behind him though, hoping no one had noticed the way they had started to shake.

"Well, in that case, why don't you take my hand and ask me to dance." Katie stood before him, her eyes never leaving his. Everything about her made it very clear she was not about to accept anything aside from agreement from Kravin.

Kravin took a second, forcing his hands to stop shaking. Once they had stopped, he lowered his head in a graceful bow and extended his hand. "Katie, my dear, would you do me the honor of dancing with me?" His hair had moved forward, covering his face, hiding the fact that he had closed his eyes tightly. Kravin fully expected her to decline his invitation out of spite for him.

To his surprise he felt the silkiness of her flash as she lightly placed her hand in his. "I would love to." Katie smiled for the first time since seeing Kravin.

As Kravin stood up, the two of them took hold of each other as they began to dance. At first Kravin, placed his hand on the curve of her hip with one other hand extended out, holding hers. It was Katie though who felt that this was not enough for the two of them. Instead, she moved close to him, eliminating the gap between the two, wrapping her small arm around the neck of Kravin. In turn, Kravin had no choice but to wrap his arm around the small waist of Katie.

Kravin could do nothing to stop the thoughts that ran through his mind as the two began to dance. Thoughts of the past the two had shared, the joy that she had brought to his life. Standing here on the dance floor, the memory of the first time she had taken his hand those many years ago—how he had prayed with all his heart that she would not, and how he quickly changed his mind the second she did take his hand—that feeling had come back to him now, the feeling he first felt that day.

He could feel the tears begin to well up in his eyes as he thought about how natural it was for him to be holding not just her hand but her. How it was like his hand had finally found its place in the world the second she had taken his. Even though she had taken his hand that day, it wasn't due to love or feelings for him, instead she had simply done it so that she would not get lost as they moved through the crowd. To her it was nothing more than a simple gesture between friends. At that time, she had no idea how it had felt to him and how it would affect him in the future.

The memories all came back to him now, memories he had tried desperately to forget for so long. Memories of a simple kiss shared one evening as she was leaving. With it a regret that he had only given her a quick peck on the lips instead of embracing her and kissing her as a lover and not a friend. So many regrets came with the memories he had of this woman, and yet somehow they still brought him happiness.

"Is everything OK, Kravin?" Katie's smile was just as sweet as he had remembered as she spoke to him. Her smile was to him like a rare gem that he could look at for hours. Together with the physical beauty that she possessed, Kravin could spend all of eternity simply taking in every inch of the angel that was now in his arms.

"Sorry, I am fine, just remembering," He fought the tears that were held just below the surface of his eyes as he spoke to her. He knew that if allowed to come forth, they would fall like rain before her. Given her chosen attire, he would not allow his strange version of tears to ruin the gown she had worn this night. No, he would not allow himself to ruin yet another thing of hers.

"So how have you been?" Katie leaned back slightly as she spoke, meeting his gaze. She smiled a little more seeing how this man was on the verge of tears as he danced with her.

"I have been doing well. All of us have been doing well actually." Kravin refused to turn away from this woman as he spoke to her. She deserved that small gesture of love and respect from him, and he would not deny her this.

"That's good, although I have already spoken with Dawg and Cher. I was just curious how you have been. It has been a long time since the two of us have seen each other." Her eyes shone in the light. Kravin could not help but notice this, and to him he thought that she too may be on the verge of tears. But there was no way this could be true. After all he had done to this woman, there was no way she would.

"Oh, sorry, yes, I have been well." Kravin looked at Katie intently, all his willpower being used to keep himself steady and respectful to this woman. He would not allow himself to ruin this moment of magic between the two.

"I would like to apologize to you and Cher though. I was curious if you were here, but I didn't intend to dance with you, to be honest. I saw that Cher walked away though as I came in, so I figured I would at least say hello." She turned her face from Kravin as she spoke; nervousness had come to her voice as well. "I guess you and Cher have become a little closer over the years, huh?"

"What do you mean closer? Cher has always been like a sister to me. You already knew that much about the two of us." The nervousness that Kravin had felt left him as she made her observation known to him.

"Well, it looked like you two were a little more than sister and brother. To be honest, the way you two were dancing, it was as if . . . you had become lovers." Katie hesitated for a moment as she spoke these final words to Kravin.

"What! No, that isn't it at all. Yes, we were dancing close when you came in, but it isn't like that, Katie. I will not lie to you though, Cher does have strong feelings for me, and if not for certain circumstances, I would feel the same for her. It pains me to say it though, but I cannot have those feelings for her. I am grateful to her though. The way she feels is something that I am not deserving of." Kravin, realizing that Cher had moved from the dance floor, looked around for the woman.

"She walked away when I came in, Kravin. It's actually kind of rude that you didn't notice. You had better go and apologize to her, but not right now, if you don't mind." Katie smiled at him as she spoke to him; she allowed a few tears to stream down her face as she looked into the eyes of Kravin yet again.

Kravin's eyes go wide as he saw the tears that fell from her eyes. His heart jumped to his throat as he realized that the woman standing before him still holds the feelings for him that she had before. "I would never leave you alone like that." Kravin winced in pain as he spoke these words, knowing that this single statement was, in truth, nothing more than a lie. He had left this woman alone once already.

Katie did not know exactly how to react to the words Kravin had just spoken to her. She knew in her heart that these words were the truth of his heart. Yet he had already proven that his mind controlled his actions and that these words were a lie. Instead of acknowledging the falseness of his statement, she instead lowered her head and placed it on his chest. Again, a woman stood in Kravin's embrace, listening to the rhythmic thump of his heart.

"I'm sorry." Kravin did not know how what he had said affected her, but he did know that he needed to apologize. Not for the words he had just spoken to her or for lying to her. No, this apology was for the actions he had taken those years ago. He had pushed his love for them to the side and instead allowed his mind to make the decisions for his future.

"Do me a favor? Once this dance is through, go and find Cher and apologize to her. She is a wonderful woman and doesn't deserve to wait as long as I have for an apology. Once you have done that, come back here and we will go somewhere and talk." The strength that Katie once carried in her eyes had left now. Replaced by a look of pleading, she wanted nothing from this man but to speak with him.

"It's a promise." Kravin pulled the delicate woman closer to him as he spoke these words. It had been so long since he had held anyone this close. Again, the feeling of belonging came to him, the feeling that this was his place. He had no idea what would be said later this night, but he hoped beyond hope that it would not be words of anger or hatred.

CHAPTER 14

Katie and Kravin had finished their dance, and as promised, Kravin left the woman with Bear and Destriga. He had promised to come back once he had found and given his apologies to Cher. Their hands lingered together as he began to walk away, his gaze never leaving her eyes. The love that had once roared like a forest fire between the two had slowly began to kindle once again.

"Well, Katie, you look as lovely as ever tonight." Bear took Katie's hand, turning her around as he spoke, allowing him and any other who was watching to see the grand beauty she was.

"Thanks, Bear, I would say the same for you, but you and Des both look like shit, to be honest." Bear could not help but smile as the tomboy he knew had come back.

"Well, in our defense, we don't exactly have the same assets as you. We have to try and convince Kravin to stay with our words where you on the other hand; well?" Destriga moved his hand up and down, pointing at Katie as he spoke.

"Well, I may have the assets that is true. But I don't have to use them either. Also I would like to point out that apparently, my assets—as you call them—must not be that great because he did leave once already." Katie placed her hand on her hip as she spoke to Destriga, amplifying the attitude in her voice.

"Yeah, you're right, and sorry for bringing it up, Katie I meant it as a joke." Destriga lowered his brow a little as he apologized to Katie.

"It's OK, Des, I know you didn't mean anything by it." Katie patted Destriga on the shoulder as she spoke to the man, reassuring him that she had taken no offense by his comment.

"Katie, I have a question for you. I don't know if you have the time or if you are willing to give it a shot, but as you can tell, Destriga and I have a small problem. I for one think you might be able to help us out. I don't want to get into it here, but sometime tomorrow, I would like for you to come to the room so we can discuss it a little further." Bear's face was stern as he spoke to the woman.

"Yeah, I can do that, Bear. I am not sure if I can help with whatever your problem is, but I will definitely give it a try." Katie smiled at Bear, trying to reassure him and give him some comfort.

"Thanks, and try not to tell Kravin. I am not sure how he would react if he knew you were involved." Bear quickly looked around him, hoping that Kravin was not close enough to hear him.

He did not notice the small figure that was standing a few feet from him. None of the three who stood talking heard the small giggle that left Ta's mouth as she slipped away into the shadows of the room and disappeared.

It did not take Kravin long to find Cher in the crowd of people. As Kravin came near her, it was obvious that she had chosen to change her attire from the intoxicating gown to her usual armor. She, however, decided not put on the various pieces of metal attire that would normally accompany it. It did not matter to Kravin though; he knew the beauty of this woman.

He did not know just how she would react to him as he came near. It didn't really matter to him at this point though. He simply stilled his nerves, making sure that nothing would prevent him from keeping the promise he had made to Katie. He also wanted to apologize to this woman once again with all his heart. He knew she deserved the love he could not give her, yet she stayed by his side regardless.

"Cher, do you have minute?" His voice was low but confident; he had no intentions of backing out now.

"Yeah, sure." Cher set down her mug and quickly stood, looking at Kravin, waiting for him to lead her in a direction.

The two of them walked out of the hall into the now-empty street. The sun had already set by this time. The streets were dimly light by torches that had been placed along them earlier in the day. The shops that normally were filled with people talking now sat silent, waiting for the morning and coming day. A single figure stood out in the moonlight aside from the two who had just exited the hall. Lady, the great beast, sat atop the wall over the gates of the Garden. Its great form posed, waiting for anything that may be considered a threat.

"Funny, that dog is so good to me. I didn't have to tell her to stay up there. She simply did it on her own." His smile was heavy as he looked at the beast. He did not have the heart to look at Cher just yet. "Cher . . ."

Cher spoke, cutting Kravin off before he could finish his statement. "I told you this before, Kravin. I know where your heart lies, and it is not with me. Yes, it is true that it was like a dream for me as we danced, but I know it isn't reality. I have come to terms with that and to be honest, I hope someday I can find the love that you and her share. I have never expected you to change the way you feel about me. I know you love me as a sister, and I have to accept that. So please, for me, don't beat yourself up about it, OK?" Cher smiled at Kravin knowing that this great man was not as solid as others may perceive him to be.

Kravin turned to Cher, again, his bloody tears flowed from his eyes as he looked at the woman before him. He knew that it took more strength than he could ever imagine for her to say the things she had just told him. He also knew that it took even more strength for her to stay by his side as she had for all these years. Never once had she wavered in her loyalty to him through all the things she had witnessed and experienced.

He felt that such loyalty was unjustified, yet here she was, granting him such an honor. There was no way in his mind that he could not become emotional hearing her words. His smile again was one of great appreciation for the amazing woman who stood in front of him. The light from the moon caressing her face made her beauty even more awe-inspiring.

"You have been with me for a long time, Cher. I know I never really gave you a chance, but you still never turned away from me. I cannot tell you just how much I appreciate the way you have taken care of me over the years. You have put up not only with my ignorance and feebleness but also the ignorance of those two boys. You're really the strongest person I know, and I thank you with all my heart for being by my side for all these years." His smile was genuine as he spoke to Cher, never breaking eye contact even when he wiped away the tears that ran down his face.

"You're welcome, brother, and I am sorry as well. I should not have put you in that position. I know how you feel, and it was disrespectful to you and Katie for me to act the way I did." Cher kept the smile on her face as she said these words. "It's over and done with, and there is no changing the way things are. So just forget about it and move on. As for me, I plan on going back in here and having a few more drinks. Besides that, I have to make sure those idiot soldiers aren't breaking the rules I had set for them."

Cher turned and opened the door to the hall. As she began to enter it, she said something under her breath that she did not realize Kravin would hear. Or at the least hoped he would not notice her saying. Kravin, however, saw her words and heard them loud and clear as she spoke them. They were words that he would hold in his heart for a long time.

Kravin chose not to address what she had said but instead allowed her to leave and rejoin the fun inside the hall. This was the least he could do for her by not acknowledging what it was that she had said when she left. He watched as she disappeared behind the doors of the great hall. He did not know whether to smile or not, but what he did know was that if Cher could live knowing how she felt, then he too would have to be strong enough to live with it as well.

For now though, he had made his apology as he had promised to Katie, and now it was time for him to find Katie and have the talk that he dreaded more than ever. How could he have let himself get put in this position? When he decided to return to the city, he had told himself he would avoid her at all costs. Yet here he was, moving through the crowd of people in the hall, looking for the woman he truly loved with all his heart.

What would she have to say to him after all these years? She seemed to still feel the same way as he did while they danced, but that could have just been for show. He had learned over the years that this woman was more than capable of hiding her true feelings behind a smile. He did not know just how he would handle what she had to say to him but what he did know was that no matter what she says, she has every right to feel the way she does.

It did not take him long to find her though. She was standing almost exactly where he had left her. She was talking with Destriga and Bear and looked to be enjoying herself. "OK, Katie, I made my apology to her." Kravin smiled with pride as he said these words. He was not sure if Katie would believe him or not but he wanted to say it anyway for his own sake.

"OK, good. Now it is my turn to have a few moments alone with you and have the conversation I told we would be having the first time we met." Her look was no longer the one of playfulness but now had turned into one of seriousness. Kravin had no idea as to what was going to happen next, but he stilled his will as the two began to walk away from Destriga and Bear.

The two moved through the hall, leaving it and the people who were enjoying the night's celebration. They walked down a few short streets before entering the castle. Kravin could not help but wonder where exactly was Katie taking him and why so far away. Regardless of this, he was willing to accept whatever it was that she had decided.

Soon they had entered the castle passing through the corridors and archways that weaved through the grand building like a maze. It was not long after entering the castle that Kravin finally figured out what Katie had in mind. She did not have some elaborate plan for him or some kind of vengeance waiting for him. No, instead she simply had chosen a spot for them to talk. A spot that was just as dear to him as it was to her.

It only took them a few minutes to find the balcony that he had wandered to earlier in the day. Instantly, being here with her brought back many memories of a time long ago. He hesitated a little before leaving the hallway that led to the balcony. Kravin watched as Katie stepped out into the moonlight. Again, he could not help but think of this woman as an angel.

The pale blue light of the moon surrounded her as she stood on the balcony, looking back at him. The white gown she had been wearing became transparent, revealing the entrancing curves of her body. It was a dream to Kravin, so much so he found himself pinching his own hand in hopes of waking up. Nothing happened though; this was no dream but reality.

Katie smiled at Kravin and waved for him to come closer to her. "Well, are you going to stand in there all night or are you going to come out here and talk to me?" Her voice was as sarcastic as ever as she beckoned for him to come to her.

"Oh, sorry, I just couldn't help but notice that your dress is kind of thin." Kravin looked Katie in the eyes as he said this. Kravin willed himself to look only at the eyes of the woman who stood before him, doing his best to treat her with all the respect he felt she deserves.

Hearing this, Katie finally looked down at the gown she was wearing and, for the first time, realized just how thin the material was. Quickly, she covered herself as her cheeks become the color of bright apples. Seeing this, Kravin quickly removed the battered jacket that he had been wearing, throwing it around the woman in order to keep her decent.

"Thanks, but you could have told me a little sooner. You know I don't like wearing stuff like this especially stuff that is pretty much see-through. Although I could have sworn the material was heavier than this." Katie pulled the jacket around her, noticing the various pieces of string that hung from it. She closed her eyes for a moment as well, remembering a time when she would wear his jacket quite often.

"Well, it wasn't like that in the hall. You know I would have said something if you were walking around flashing everybody." Kravin's tone was firm and reassuring as he spoke to her.

"Yeah, I know, but that would only be if you noticed. And I have told you before, you are kind of captain oblivious." The smirk returning to her face as she spoke added to the sarcasm in her voice.

"Yeah well, trust me, I would have noticed if your dress wasn't exactly leaving anything to the imagination." Kravin couldn't help but feel like things were exactly the same as they were in the past. Like nothing had changed between the two of them.

Katie did not respond to him this time, instead she moved closer to him, taking his arm. The two stood for a moment, looking off into the distance. The pair stood locked in memories of a joyous past. Memories of laughter and arguments, passion and understanding; they both stood smiling off into the distance, neither of them knowing just what to say to the other. Yet they both knew that something must be said. They must have this conversation; otherwise, things will never get better for either of them.

With all that, Kravin also knew that with this conversation there will also be a decision to be made. The more time he spent with Katie, he could tell that she still loved him just as much as she had before. To her, nothing had changed between them. She still wore the ring he had given her. Even this place was special and, to her, the perfect place for them to have the coming discussion.

"You're going to leave us again, aren't you?" Katie looked at him, doing her best to force a smile as she looked at him.

"I wish I could say no that I am going to stay, but that would be a lie. You and I both know that the consequences of me staying are too great. On top of that, it would seem that this whole thing has been nothing but a ruse to get me out in the open. So even if I leave, all of you will still be in danger. To be honest, right now, I am lost. For the first time in all these years, I do not have the answer to the problem that is sitting right in front of me." Kravin did not return the gaze of Katie as he spoke. He was afraid of seeing her face as he spoke these words to her.

"Well, if the danger is going to be here whether you are here or not, then why not stay? Kravin, come home, we miss you so much. I miss you." The smile Katie had fought so hard to put on no longer appeared on her face.

"I can't stay. I cannot have everyone in this city be subject to this kind of danger just because of my selfishness." Kravin finally looked down at the woman who stood by his side. He never really understood how this woman could cause him so much pain yet bring him the greatest joy at the same time.

"Why? You think that if you stay, everyone is just going to die? Do you really believe that you bring that kind of danger with you?" Katie's voice no longer carried the weight of sadness but instead hinted at anger. She did not know how the man in front of her could act so differently at the same time.

"You know exactly why I can't stay. If I lose control again, who knows what might happen. I can't take that risk. I cannot put you guys in that kind of danger. I also could not bear it if I hurt any of you." Kravin could not help but show the fear that had been haunting him for so long as he said this.

"You couldn't bear to hurt us. What do you think you are doing not being here with us? You think it is all rainbows and sunshine knowing the man that I love refuses to be with me yet tells me he loves me more than anything in the world?" Katie pulled away from Kravin, her fury had taking control at this point.

"What am I supposed to do, come here and risk hurting you if I lose control, or stay away and make sure that never happens but hurt you emotionally instead of physically?" Kravin's once-proud stature had left him now. His shoulder hung low as he spoke, his back slightly bent; it was obvious to anyone who saw him that this was the true nature of this man.

"I don't know what you are supposed to do, Kravin. What I do know is that there are people here who love and care about you. People who are willing to help you stay in control of your power and learn to control it so you don't have to worry anymore." Katie managed to quell her anger, again pleading with the man she loved.

"CONTROL IT! There is no controlling it, don't you get it? I have spent the last fifty years trying to learn to control it, but there is nothing I can do. There is no amount of learning that I can do to keep this power under control. It isn't just the power, Katie, it's the demons that reside in my mind that are the problem. My own weakness is the reason I cannot control this power." Kravin could do nothing at this point but try with all his might not to fall to his knees before Katie. The torture of his power and the sacrifices he had chosen to make because of it had come to bare on him full force.

"You are my husband, for better or for worst, till death do us part. I agreed to those terms and so did you. You talked so great before you had this power, about how you would do anything for me, and how you would never betray or leave me. Now look at you . . . you can barely stand in front of me." Katie placed her hand on the side of Kravin's face as she spoke. "You were the strongest man I knew, my love. What has happened to you? I watched as you fought to get where you were before the flare. After the flare, you seemed to be the same man as before. Now, though, the longer you have lived with this power, you allow yourself to be controlled by the incident so long ago."

This was all Kravin could take; the words spoken by Katie carried with them the weight of a thousand worlds. It was a weight that Kravin could no longer carry; his legs buckled and he fell to his knees in front of the woman he loved. "It isn't just what I did but what I saw in my mind that day that haunts me. I saw my own reflection in my mind, and it was the devil himself. I refuse to give him the opportunity to take everything away from me."

"So instead, you choose to give it all up before he can take it from you?" Katie's voice was harsh yet still carried a hint of understanding for Kravin.

"No, that isn't it at all . . ." Kravin did not get the chance to finish what he was going to say.

"Then fight, my husband, fight for me, fight for us, fight for your city. Once you are done fighting, then come back to me." Katie turned and walked toward the doorway that had led to the balcony. "When you are done with your fighting, you can come get your jacket back, you know where it will be." Katie did not wait for Kravin to respond as she walked through the doorway and turned down the corridor. She refused to wipe away the tears that streaked her face because they were not tears of sadness but tears of hope. Hope that Kravin would be able to fight not only this battle but his own demons and come back to her.

Kravin sat back on his knees after Katie had left him. He stared up into the night sky, entranced by the stars that hung like jewels above the city. "What am I supposed to do, Lord? I am not sure if you were the mind behind the way things are now, but if you are, please help me. I want nothing more than to be with her and everyone, but I am not strong enough to fight the devil inside me alone."

CHAPTER 15

The celebration had continued long into the night. Destriga and Bear stayed as long as the people of the Garden felt the need to release the energy they had. They wanted to stay to be a sign of hope for their people. It was a sight that the two men had miss seeing. All the people of the city had spent the last few weeks in fear doing only what had to be done. This night, however, they could rejoice and be free from the burdens, and it had gone just that way.

"Well, Des, to be honest, I think that went pretty well tonight. From what I can tell, the people had enjoyed the celebration, and Cher only had to give a few of the soldiers the riot act." Bear clapped Destriga on the shoulder as he spoke.

"Yeah, I would have to agree tonight did go well. The thing I am really worried about is how things are going to go in the morning. I realize the people really needed this, but I am not sure if it was the best time for us to be celebrating. We won a battle, sure, but we have been winning battles all week." Destriga allowed a frown to take over his face for just an instant as he spoke.

"Yeah, that is true, but to be honest, we haven't really been winning battles—not like we did today. The majority of battles we won"—Bear held his hands up, making a quoting motion as he spoke—"aren't because we won but because the Oritha had simply decided they were done fighting for the day. Today, though, we actually won. As long as Kravin and the others can keep pushing them back, I think we have a good chance of actually winning this war."

"You are right. We have not really won any of the battles that have taken place so far in this war. You are also right that as long as Kravin and his people are here, we should have no problem in ending this war in our favor. The only thing that really strikes my curiosity, though, is why did someone decide that it was necessary to go through all this trouble just to get Kravin out of the fortress and back here? I keep going over it in my mind, but I cannot, for the life of me, think of anyone who would really know about his power or him." Destriga looked toward Bear as spoke, allowing his confusion to show.

"Well, we can either sit here or wonder what the motive is and who is behind it, or we can get our strength back and go to whoever it is and find out for ourselves. The three of us together have never come across anything or anyone that we could not overcome. The only problem with that is you and I are on the short end of the stick when it comes to getting our powers back, and Kravin— well, he is too afraid to use his own power." Bear smiled, hoping it would bring his friend some comfort and inspire him to figure out the more important problems first.

"Well, I guess that means I need to stop worrying about it and start trying to figure out a way for us to get our strength back." Destriga finally returned the smile of his friend.

"Yep, and we can leave Kravin to Katie. I am sure that woman will be able to get his ass back in gear in no time at all." Bear clapped Destriga on the back a little harder this time, moving the small man forward.

"Well, speaking of the woman of the hour, it would seem Katie and Kravin are done talking." Destriga pointed to the entrance of the hall, showing Bear that Katie had just returned to the celebration.

Katie did not stop to speak with anyone as she moved through the crowd. As before, when she first entered the hall, anyone who had been standing in front of the woman moved to the side subconsciously. This reaction was always something that made her slightly nervous, even more so after finding out that her dress was almost transparent. She pulled the jacket that Kravin had given her tightly around her. As she did, she could not help the feelings that rushed into her mind as his scent filled her nose.

The memories of so many days spent together filled her mind. Carefree evenings that had come and gone, leaving only trace memories to comfort her now. With those memories, she could not help but remember the nights of passion that came after those evenings. It wasn't just the physical passion that had brought her joy but the emotional passion as well. It was those times that she knew that he lived only for her. Yet now it seemed as if he lived for no one, like he almost wished for death to release him from the burden that had been placed upon him.

Destriga and Bear could see that the conversation may not have gone as well as they had hoped it would. The expression on Katie's face was one of confusion, anger, and sadness all rolled together. It was also a surprise to them both that she had not chosen to retire for the night but instead came to them in order to help them with their problem.

"All right, you two said you wanted my help with something. So let's go and see if I can do anything to help you." The mix of emotions that had painted her face previously had vanished and instead was replaced with a look of determination.

"Well, no offense, but it is kind of late, Katie. We can look into it tomorrow if you would prefer. We are in a hurry, but it is still important for you and us to get as much rest as possible." Destriga knew that this would not deter the woman from her mission, but he wanted to try either way.

"You are right, we all need are rest, but it looks to me that rest isn't really doing either one of you any good now, is it? I assume that is what you two want my help with, right? So if that is the case, then I say we do it right now and see if I can do anything to help you two recover your strength." Katie did not care how they would respond to this. Instead, she simply moved toward the door that would lead to the castle.

"Well, Des, I am not sure if this is a good thing or a bad thing. Either way though, I think we had better do as she says." Bear allowed a broad grin to cover his face as he followed the woman to the door.

"Something tells me this is yet another thing that is not going to end all that well for either of us, or Kravin for that matter." Destriga too turned and began moving the direction of Katie and Bear.

The three of them moved through the doorway leading to the castle. It did not take them long to move through the corridors to the room. It had been a long time since Katie had set foot in this room. It was not because she was not welcome; in fact, she was one of the few people who could enter here without being invited first by one of the three founders of this city.

She found it hard to do anything since Kravin had left her. Why she chose to do anything at this moment, she did not really know. It was possible that she hoped if she did do something that Kravin would stay. The one thing she did know, however, was that if she did nothing to help these two men, then the only hope they had was of Kravin and those that followed him. She did not have any doubts that Cher and Dawg were more than capable of defending this city, but there was something in the air.

She had felt it the first night the fighting had started, but she could not pinpoint what it was that sent a chill down her spine. There was an evil out there that was hungry for battle—not just battle but for chaos. Katie was sure that this may be the one reason that whatever or whoever it was that had gone to such lengths to pull Kravin from his exile. If that was the case, she also knew that if Kravin were to unleash his full power, that feeling that force of chaos would take hold and do whatever it could to drive him mad.

She could not believe that she had just figured this out. Not because she felt she was not capable of it but because she did not normally think in this way. It did not really matter right now though. She needed to help Destriga and Bear to regain their power in order to help Kravin in the battle that she was sure was going to take place. He would need their strength as well as the strength of all his friends to keep him from losing control.

That single thought brought back another thing she had tried to forget over the years. It was something she had hoped she would never have to use. Yet something told her that it was more important than ever for her to go and retrieve the possession she had long since forgotten. Katie knew where she had hidden it, but could she still get there? And if so, would it still be there?

The thought too sent a chill down her spine, the thought that someone other than herself would have access to it. She had never thought about this before, being distracted by the happiness of the time and the sadness that had taken its place. Katie quickly dismissed the idea that someone could have found it. Kravin himself could not find it, and he was very good at that sort of thing.

Katie chose to ignore this particular thought and the thoughts that went along with it. It was a memory and an idea that she did not want to think about at this time. Instead, she turned her attention to the men who stood before her. "I assume that you two are hoping that I can heal the two of you, and in turn, it will replenish the strength that you cannot regain on your own?"

Destriga was the first to respond to Katie. "Actually, that was the general idea, yes." Destriga was not the least bit surprised that Katie had already figured out what it was that the two of them had been planning on trying. Bear nodded in agreement with Destriga as the two looked at Katie.

"Well then, what are we waiting for?" Katie, seeing that both Destriga and Bear were eager to be the experiment, took the hands of Destriga. Closing her eyes, Katie began to focus on the man in front her. As she did this, a golden light began to engulf her and then flow into Destriga. Bear stood watching as the light expanded between the two, and he saw something he had not expected.

As the light moved from Katie to Destriga, he saw what appeared to be a wall of blackness that seemed to start at the wrists of Destriga and emanate outward, preventing the light from flowing completely to him. It was obvious to him that there was something very powerful that was keeping them from regaining their strength. He also noted that even in this room, a place that had been split from the reality that they knew, the power still had full affect.

Katie and Destriga stood for several minutes as she used her power, but it seemed to have no effect on Destriga. Realizing this, she allowed the light that had engulfed her to subside and let go of him. Hoping for the best, she turned to Bear, extending her hands. "Well, big guy, let's see if you are any different." Bear took the small hands of Katie; it was at times like these he fully understood why they had chosen to call him Bear. His hands looked like the size of bear paws as he held the hands of Katie.

Again, Katie conjured the golden light, engulfing herself in it as she had with Destriga. Again, the light slowly began to move toward Bear. Destriga was the one who saw the wall of blackness on Bear. As it did with him, the wall expanded from his wrists outward, preventing the light from reaching Bear. Katie did not hold the light as long this time. Instead, she chose to end it very quickly.

"Well, it would seem that is not going to work. I do have another thing I would like to try if you two are up for it though." Her voice showed no signs of despair; instead, it seemed to be full of hope. "Honestly, I am pretty sure this is going to work. The only problem is, I am not sure how well or how it will affect me."

"What do you mean you are not sure how it will affect you?" Destriga looked at Katie, puzzled by her statement.

"Well, to be honest, somehow, whoever did this to the two of you has blocked your, um, let's say, life force. When I heal someone, I simply boost their life force energy, which causes their body to heal itself and recuperate. Which is why it doesn't work on you two, someone has blocked your life force. That is the best way I can think of on how to explain how this works." Katie smiled brightly as she spoke to Bear and Destriga. She always got some self-satisfaction when she got to explain something new to Kravin, Destriga, or Bear. As long as she had known the three men, there seemed to be very little they did not know or understand quickly.

"OK, so if our life force is blocked and your powers simply amplify a life force, then how exactly are you going to fix us?" Bear did not seem too perplexed by Katie but instead appeared curious and excited at the same time.

"Well, I have another way to heal. It is the only way that I learned how to heal Kravin, to be honest. The only problem is that he made me promise to never use it on anyone especially him." Katie turned her gaze from both Bear and Destriga as she said this. She did not want to tell the men how exactly it worked. She knew that if they knew, they would not allow her to try it out of respect for Kravin.

"OK, now I am a little cautious on whether I want to let you do it or not, Katie. If Kravin thinks it is that dangerous, that you should not do it to even him, then it is almost certainly out of the question." Destriga spoke sternly to Katie, knowing that his friend loved this woman more than anyone. He could not allow her to do something that Kravin had already deemed unsafe for her.

"Look, right now, Kravin does not matter, OK. Actually, on the other hand, he does matter. You know as well as I do that he is afraid of his own power. As long as he is afraid of his power, then he may lose control again. Which also means if he has to use his power and loses control, then it will take all that we have to stop him again. So right now, I don't care whether he likes it or not. He may be my husband, but he does not make my decisions. I do. So if I say it is worth it, then it is worth it." The look of Katie was one both Destriga and Bear had seen multiple times before, except they normally saw it on the face of their friend and not his wife.

"Well, aside from all that—which I would have to agree with you, Katie, that if he does lose control again, it will take everything we have to stop him—I would also like to add that you and he have spent way too much time together. That look was the look he has given us countless times, and it would seem to have rubbed off." Bear smiled at Katie, clasping her on the shoulder, letting her know that he supported her decision.

"Thanks, Bear, but just you know this was my look first. He stole it." She smiled as she looked at the two men. Destriga did not respond but instead took hold of Katie's hands. He nodded to her, letting her know that it was time for her to try her second method.

Katie did not waste time in her second attempt with Destriga. Again, Bear saw as the golden light began to emanate from Katie; only this time, it was not an aura that formed around her but instead a stream of light that came directly from her heart. As the light moved out away from Katie, Bear could see that this type of healing was not just different, but it was just as dangerous as Kravin had claimed.

The light was not just a generic light as before, but in it, Bear could see what appeared to be memories in the light. Thoughts, idea, and emotions from Katie herself, all of them moved in the light as they fanned out above her. More and more light poured out from the heart of this woman until it looked like a pair of enormous wings. As Bear watched, he found himself paralyzed in awe at the power this woman had in her.

It took only a minute before Bear could see an effect on Katie. He breathing had hastened, and her once-tanned skin had started to become pale. This light was exactly what Bear had thought. It was not simply a light of energy, but it was Katie's own life force that he was seeing. "Katie, you have to stop now!" was all Bear could say as he watched the wings of light envelope Destriga.

Instantly, Katie let go of Destriga and fell to the floor. Bear, seeing her fall instantly, went to her side, checking for a pulse. He heaved a sigh of relief when he found that she was still alive. Her pulse was weak, and her eyes were closed; he knew she had fainted from what she had just done.

"Bear, what happened? Why did you tell her to stop?" Destriga seemed to be panicked at the situation seeing Katie on the floor, unconscious.

"You have no idea what she just did?" Bear was surprised that Destriga could not tell. He was even more surprised that what Katie had just done actually worked. "You couldn't tell that she was giving you her own life force?"

"What do you mean giving me her life force?" Destriga, seeing that Katie had begun to stir, moved to grab a chair and slid it closer to her.

"He's right, Des. It was the only thing I could think of to do, and look—it worked." Though it was obvious she was very weak, Katie managed to smile at the results of her efforts.

Destriga, who had looked feeble and tired when he entered the chamber, instead looked as he had always been. His complexion had returned to the normal tan he used to have. The muscle of his body that was almost invisible beneath his clothing had returned. Katie had given Destriga the strength and power back that he had always had.

"I have to say this though, guys. Even if I do this for you, Bear, there is no guarantee that it is a permanent fix. I can give you guys a boost for now, but if you use the power, it will be gone." The smile that had crossed the face of Katie never left as she told the two men this. "On the other hand, as long as you come to me, I can keep giving you boosts."

"No," Bear and Destriga both responded to Katie at the same time. Their tones were more serious than she had heard in a long time. "You are not going to give me a boost unless it is absolutely necessary. The same goes for Destriga. You use your life force to help us, and to be honest, who knows if you even get it back. No, Katie, this is just as dangerous as Kravin said. This is going to be the first and last time you do this unless we have to." Bear did not change his tone as he spoke with Katie. He did not want her risking her life to help them, not only because he cared for her as a friend, but he also knew that if anything happened to Katie, there would be no one who could stop the wrath of Kravin.

"Agreed, so for now, we will stay here until you get your strength back, then you are going home and getting some rest." Destriga slid a chair over to Bear and pulled one up for himself. Snapping his fingers together, the fire in the middle of the table again roared to life.

"Huh, I give you my life and you waste it to light a fire?" Katie smiled at Destriga as she said her joke.

"Actually, this would be Kravin's life force. Yours is way more valuable." Destriga stared into the flames as he spoke.

Bear and Katie too found themselves entranced by the fire that raged in the middle of the table. Katie knew that Destriga was not using his power to conjure these flames, but instead it was a gift of sorts from Kravin to him. She could not help but remember the day those flames first came into existence. She had never seen him be pushed as far as Destriga pushed him that day. It was still astonishing that Kravin had not killed him, but she also knew that Destriga was trying to help the two of them by getting Kravin to direct his anger at him.

CHAPTER 16

That day was a very interesting one as Katie remembered it. It was toward the end when Kravin had chosen to leave the Garden and all of them behind. She never really did figure out what it was that had pushed him so far prior to meeting with them in this place. Katie had not spent much of the day with him. Instead, she had been running errands up until the time for them to meet.

When she arrived, Kravin had an attitude that she had seen before. More than one time prior to the flare, she had dealt with him in the same kind of mood. This time though seemed to be different. Normally, she remembered him keeping to himself and not speaking to anyone whenever he got into one of his moods. Instead, he seemed to speak to everyone. Maybe it was because he was trying to get help. That was one of the things that he had a lot of problems with his entire life, asking for help when he really needed it.

He had no problems asking for help when it was petty, like lifting something or doing anything physical. On the opposite end, if he had any emotional problems, he would simply bottle it up and not talk to anyone, which would normally make it worse. It seemed to her that day was something of the same. She expected him to bottle it up and simply ignore everyone as he would normally do for a few days and then everything would be back to normal.

Katie looked at Destriga as she went through the events in her head. Destriga and Bear both seemed to have noticed something different about his bad mood this time though. Katie remembered that she had started scolding him for some reason she did not know why. She guessed that it has probably something to do with him acting the way he was. Destriga and Bear both saw what was happening though.

Katie thought to herself how she could not believe that she did not notice his anger building as quickly as it did. Katie knew that no matter what, Kravin would never allow himself to attack her; but in all the years she had known him, she truly felt that it was a possibility that day. She was sure that Bear and Destriga probably thought the same thing. They both noticed that something was off about him that day and took action.

Katie did not confuse herself about who they were really trying to save that day. Both of these great men who sat with her cared for her, but Kravin was their brother. They both knew that if he had done something to hurt her, that there was no way that he would be able to live with himself. Katie could not help to think as well that perhaps those two men were more worried about what Kravin would do to everyone and everything around him had he lost control after hurting her.

Everything happened so quickly that day as they sat around the table. Destriga had said something, yet as hard as she tried to remember what exactly it was that he had said to Kravin, she could not. What she did remember was what happened next. The center of the table exploding with a burst of energy, that ominous black light that shone from the eyes of her husband as he leapt across the table at Destriga.

In turn, Destriga quickly blinked, instantly teleporting himself from the chair he was on to a few inches behind it, evading Kravin. That began the game of cat and mouse between the two of them. Kravin never used his true power as they fought; his fingers became sharp talons that tore at every inch of this room. As Katie remembered the events of the night, her eyes moved from one spot in the room to the next. The scars in the walls, pillars, floor, and even the ceiling, backing up every second of the memory she relived.

The sight of Kravin in this state had been etched into her memory. If anything, she knew that this is one thing she would never forget. In the end, it took Bear restraining him and Katie doing everything in her power to calm her husband to stop the war that was being raged in this small room. What had happened afterwards she did not expect.

As Kravin came out of the state he had been in while fighting, his body seemed to lose its strength. In the end, it seemed as if he could barely hold his own weight as he stood before Katie, Bear, and Destriga. He never really apologized to Destriga or Bear for the events of that night; instead, he simply conjured the flame in the center of the table. His words sent chills down her spine as Katie remembered them.

The tone of his voice and the look on his face were not the Kravin she knew. He had always spent a lot of his time in a serious manner. Nothing in this world that he did or anyone he knew was ever taken lately. Every relationship was precious to him, yet that day, as he stood and spoke those words it was like all the emotion had left him. As if he was no more than a dead husk that moved and spoke without feeling.

"As long as this flame burns red, then you know that I am still me. If it were to ever turn black as the eyes you see before, you then I pray that you can stop me." He looked at the three of them, making sure that each of them could see his eyes. She had always been drawn to his eyes for some reason; there was nothing really special to them. They were brown or hazel at times, yet they always seemed to show how he was feeling. Some people say he wore his emotions on his sleeve, but in reality, his emotions were always in his eyes.

At that moment though, his eyes did not have that warm glow to them that had always drawn her closer to him. No, at that moment, there was no warmth in his eyes or emotion. They were black as the abyss. Had it not been for the light of the fire reflecting off them, it would have appeared that his eyes were no longer there. What was it that had caused this change in him? How long would her husband have to fight to keep control?

Katie's thoughts and memories drifted in out of her mind as she succumbed to the fatigue of helping Destriga. The two men who sat with her watched as the woman drifted into slumber. Both of them knew that there was only one thing on her mind this night. A soft whisper came from her lips as she finally let go and fell asleep. "I will always love you." Bear caught the small woman as she hunched over in her seat.

Bear and Destriga did not want to wake or disturb the woman who had just given them an emergency way out if it came to it. They both looked at each other, the expressions on their faces said all there was to say between the two men. Their friend had one of the strongest woman they knew at his side, a woman who was as willing to sacrifice herself for him as he was for her.

Now that they had discovered a short-term cure for what ailed them, they could focus on the most important part of the problem at hand: stopping this war and preventing Kravin from doing anything that may cause him to lose control once again. Neither man was sure what would trigger him to do so, but they both did know that it would be one of countless reasons. Not because they felt he was too emotional or unstable. No, it was because he held so many people dear to him that if anything were to happen to any of them, it would be a disaster.

For now, though, they would allow Katie to sleep and simply ponder the possibilities that lay before them. Once she had awaken and left to go home, than the two men would begin that discussion. They also needed to wait for their friend to return. His insight was as precious at this time as the help that Katie had just provided them.

It was then when the two men had consigned themselves to simply watching the flames before them that they noticed it. The flames that had been red for as long as they could remember had started to take on another color. Bear could see that some of the flames that reached to the ceiling of the room had become dark. Destriga did not see those but instead found himself looking at the base of the fire. It was there that he could vividly see the glow of those black flames once again.

Both men at this point began to share the same thought. Just how long had the flames been this color? More importantly, how long would it be before they once again turned the color of the abyss? Destriga flexed his right hand many times, hoping to remember something. He stared for a moment at the hex that Kravin had placed on his hand, hoping for some kind of sign that was not there.

CHAPTER 17

Katie did not know what time it was when she finally left the castle. She was glad that Bear and Destriga were not upset about waiting for her to wake up before they could leave. Although she was certain that given the circumstances of the recent event that the two men did not get much sleep. She did take some happiness knowing that she could help them regain their power to a certain extent.

She knew that by helping them, she in turn would be helping Kravin and the entire city. That was something she felt was worth any price. She had resolved herself during her conversation with her husband that she would do whatever it takes to keep the city safe and ease his burden. She just hoped that Bear and Destriga would allow her the opportunity to help.

As she walked, she noticed that it had been a very long time since she had seen the city in this light. Kravin and she would take moonlit walks through the city many nights when it was warm enough for her. It was funny how opposite they were, yet she could still see the beauty in the things she felt so passionately about. Without him, it had never been a desire for her to walk or even be up this late at night.

She could not help but miss those days, when they would view the city from points no one else could. He would take her to rooftops that gave the city almost heavenly properties as they watched. He would tell her how the best time to see the city was at its darkest hours of the night. It never really made much sense at the time. Given the last few weeks of war, it had started to become apparent as to what exactly he had meant by that. Granted, he was mainly talking about how the lights of that city gave it a glow. Yet at the same time she could not help but feel like he meant this too.

The people of this city had come together to defend it from the Oritha. Those of the city who were considered to be thieves and criminals had come to the aid of the city using their skills to do whatever they could to benefit it and the people. She herself knew that people were very strong naturally, given the things she had dealt with in her life. She did not, however, think that people could come together like this; to her, it was amazing to see it.

Katie knew that to Kravin, though, it was no miracle or amazing feat but in fact something he had always known would happen. Kravin had so much faith in the people of this city; she knew that was one of the reasons why he had left. He did not want to be the reason as to why the people of this city would band together. He did not want to be the monster in the dark.

Katie did not take long getting to her home, her thoughts slowly fading away as she came closer. She wanted only to slip into her home and lie down on the first thing she could and sleep until the morning. Though she could not help but wonder just how long that would be since she really had no idea how long she had already been asleep. She did note that it did not seem like dawn was approaching, so she hoped she had at least a few hours given the natural alarm clock of hers.

The door was locked as usual, but when she entered, it was very obvious that someone was in her home. It was a presence that had not been here in a long time, and it was one she welcomed. Katie did not move quickly as she took of the coat Kravin had given her. She felt as though it was necessary for her to take her time before she finally went to see the person who had entered her home.

Katie looked around curious if any of the pictures that were set about the house had been moved, hoping that maybe this person had taken some interest in seeing them. Katie could not help but feel a little disappointment as nothing seemed to be out of place. Seeing this, she finally decided that instead of lying down on the couch, which she felt was more comfortable than her bed, she would instead go to her room.

As Katie moved down the hallway to her room, she finally noticed the one thing that had been misplaced. The door to her room had been left open slightly; Katie smiled a little smile thinking that this must have been done on purpose. She thought to herself, wondering why he had decided to come here in the first place. Those thoughts all stopped though as she made her way to the door and opened it.

Katie stepped through the doorway of her room half-ignoring Kravin as he sat on her bed. It was obvious to her that his mood had not improved much from when she last spoke to him. "Well, it looks like you haven't managed to make any decisions yet have you?" Her tone was stern as she spoke to Kravin.

"You make it sound as if it is the easiest thing in the world to do." Kravin did not look up at his wife. His face was turned to the ground, rubbing his hands together slowly as he contemplated his coming actions.

"Well, to be honest, I would think it would be easy. You love us and everyone in the city, so it would seem to me that if you love everything here so much, then you would do whatever it takes to keep it safe." Katie could not help but remember the many nights she had spent like this with Kravin. The number of conversations the two would have as she changed her clothing. Her fondest memories, however, were the nights they would say nothing; he would simply sit and watch her. He would always say that she was too beautiful for him not to be mesmerized by her.

"If I wasn't risking everything at the same time, I would. I told you I can't risk losing control again and being the very thing that destroys this city when I am trying to save it." Kravin had finally moved his gaze from the floor to his wife. Even now in all his turmoil, he could not help but watch her. Kravin had always felt that she must have been some beautiful piece of art brought to life. Ever curve was perfect on her body, her hair soft and flowing; but with all her physical traits, it was her eyes and personality that had won his heart so long ago.

Katie too smiled as she noticed him watching her. "Ya know, it's been a while since anyone has watched me undress. To be honest, I am not sure if I really like it anymore." The smile on her face grew as she said this because she knew that it was a lie. She enjoyed it as much as he did. Not because of some weird fetish but because she knew he loved her with all his heart and soul. There was not a moment of the day he had not told her how beautiful she was.

"Sorry, to be honest, I didn't even think about it. Just being back here at this time and seeing you in the room, it felt like before. I'll go so you can get to bed, oh, and I am sorry for coming here uninvited." Kravin moved to get up from the bed, Katie stopping him as he did.

Katie stepped in front of him, knocking him back down on to the bed. "I didn't say I wanted you to leave. Geez, could you just relax for a moment? You have always been like this, always taking things so serious." Katie bent over and slid her arms around Kravin, smiling at him and looking into his eyes. "You are my husband, you may have left for a long time, but I am still your wife and this is still your house." Katie placed a kiss on Kravin's forehead as she finished her statement. "This is still your bed."

Kate pushed Kravin back on to the bed as she spoke to him. It had been a long time since anyone besides Katie had slept in this bed. She herself had not spent much time, preferring the couch most nights. Tonight, she wanted to be in this bed, to spend the night with her husband. "Stay here with me, stay with me and never let go like you promised."

Kravin did not say a word to his wife as he moved. He picked her up from the bed and pulled back the covers, laying her down gently. The two of them embraced each other as he lay down beside her. They had both missed this one feeling for so long. Not the feeling of physical intimacy, but to simply hold each other as they slept. It had been a long time since Katie had fallen asleep with a smile on her face; tonight was the night that would end that.

Katie awoke as she did every morning just as the light of the sun began to peek through her window. She smiled remembering that her husband had stayed with her. She moved to feel his body next to hers. She was not surprised, however, to find that she was the only one in the bed. For a second, she thought to herself that it may have been a dream. However, the proof that he had been there had been placed on the table near the bed. He had made her breakfast before he had left.

She could not help but feel a little upset that he had left prior to her waking up, yet at the same time, she knew why he had left. Kravin was not ready to confront the entire situation he had left for fifty years. Katie only hoped that he would find the courage to deal with it soon before it may be too late. She moved from her bed, unable to resist the smell of the toast he had made for her. The cinnamon made her mouth water; he had learned to make this French toast from his mother, and it was amazing.

Kravin had returned to the wall after leaving his home and his wife. Lady had never left the spot on the wall that she had taken the night before. He smiled at the doglike beast as he scratched her head. Lady returned his affection, licking his entire face at once. "OK, girl, you can go get some sleep. Mom should be awake, so why not go and see her. She might even have some leftovers for you to eat."

Lady did not take long to turn and began moving. At first she walked only ten or fifteen feet from Kravin before turning around to look at her master. "It's OK, I will fine, so go on." After hearing this, Lady did as she was told bounding down the stairs. Kravin heard a few startled cries as Lady ran through the streets of the city, moving toward Kravin's home.

Kravin stood looking out across the field in front of the city. The smoke that floated toward the sky in the woods beyond the field held his attention for a moment. Kravin knew that someone was behind all of this; what he could not figure out still was why. How did this person manage to gather all the Oritha together and control them? Why was it so important for them to lure him out at the cost of so many innocent people?

Again, he looked at the field knowing that in a few hours' time, the real battle would begin. Many of the soldiers of the city would lose their lives this day, no matter what happens. The biggest problem, however, for him was deciding just how many of those soldiers would be the price to use his power. He prayed that he would not have to take action himself; instead his hopes rested on his brother and friends.

Kravin's attention was diverted as Ta appeared through one of her portals. She was sitting on top of one of the wall towers, kicking her feet like a child. "Well, I haven't seen you in a few hours, Ta. Normally, you are running around, causing problems for everyone you can." His tone was playful with the woman.

"Yeah well, there is enough chaos around here at the moment. Didn't think there was a need to add to it." Ta's tone was slightly aggressive as she said this. Almost like she had been insulted by Kravin.

"Well, someone seems to be having a rather bad morning." Kravin turned to watch the soldiers as they began to gather at the gate. He noted that Cher had not cut the men a break at all when it came to the morning training.

"Yeah well, it isn't just a bad morning. To be honest, I have been trying to figure out if I wanted to tell you something or not." Ta turned her head, refusing to look at Kravin as she spoke. Instead, she fixed her gaze on the many clouds that moved over their heads.

"Hmmm, I would assume it must be something important. Yet if you think it isn't that important that you should tell me, then I guess don't worry about it." Kravin finally looked at Ta as he spoke. She appeared for the first time in a long time to be nervous for some reason.

"Yeah well, it isn't all that important to me, but it is something that is important to you." Ta looked at Kravin, not realizing that he had been looking at her. His eyes had softened since the last time she had spoken to him. Something was definitely different this morning. "I take it you went home last night, huh?"

Kravin smiled at Ta as she asked him this question. She could not believe that his gaze could soften any more than it already was, but she was wrong. "Actually yes, I did stay with Katie last night, why?"

"Well, I guess you two must have patched things up then, huh?" Ta's expression did not hide the aggravation that was obvious in her voice.

"It would seem that there was nothing to patch up. There are a lot of things that we need to discuss, but on the other hand, she understands why I left like I did." Kravin never turned away from Ta as he spoke. He instead chose to hold her gaze.

"Well, if that's the case, then I will go ahead and tell you. I followed Bear and Destriga like you asked me to. I heard them ask Katie if she could help them with something, but they didn't want you to know about it." Ta couldn't help but think that she may have made a mistake as she spoke to Kravin. His eyes, which had been very soft and inviting just a second ago, were now cold. "So I went ahead and followed her after she came back from talking to you. We ended up in the room I can't tele into. I am not sure if Bear or Destriga noticed, though I am pretty sure they didn't, given how weak they are right now. Well, Destriga isn't all that weak now. He actually had almost all his power back."

"You mean Katie did something to help Bear and Destriga regain their strength?" Kravin's eyes softened a little as he heard this.

"Yeah, but it isn't something you should be getting happy about, Kravin. She tried to use her regular healing on them, and it didn't work. It was really weird too. That light she gives off surrounded her, and then when it went to Bear or Destriga, there was like this black wall that stopped it from actually touching them. So because of that she—" Ta was cut short as she spoke.

"She used a power that looked like wings?" It was not just Kravin's eyes that went cold, but it seemed to Ta as if he started to suck the warmth from the air around him now.

"Yeah, that is exactly what she did." Ta had never expected Kravin to get as upset as he was at this moment. She had heard Katie, Bear, and Destriga talk about Kravin not being happy knowing she had used this ability, but she did not imagine he would be this angry. "Look, I just wanted to tell you." With that, Ta disappeared, not giving Kravin a chance to say any more to her. She knew that Destriga and Bear had to be told that Kravin knows what had happened.

CHAPTER 18

Kravin stood for a while, watching the field as it slumbered. He went over the plans he had been making time and time again, the possibilities of what the Oritha may do. Everything was like a puzzle to him; over and over again he tried to figure out every little detail. He was not sure as to how long he had been standing there, going over his puzzles. What he did know, however, was that the time had come.

He could hear the sound of the Oritha as they moved onto the battlefield. The thunder of the footsteps made no mistake that all of the Oritha had been mobilized for this day's battle. He had expected this of course; his opponent wanted him to display his power, and the best way for him or she to do so was to throw all of its power at him.

Destriga and Bear did not take long to show up to the wall where Kravin had been standing watch. It was all Kravin could do to not lash out at the two men who had put Katie in danger. Kravin knew though that these two men could not have known just how much it had cost Katie to heal them. Kravin did take comfort when he saw that Destriga was the only one who had been given his power back.

That meant that she may have explained it at least in light detail to them. Still they had asked her to help them with this knowing that it was something Kravin would not want happening. He felt as though these two men had just disrespected him by going behind his back and asking his wife to help them. That was something that he could not afford to think about at this time though. The battle was fast approaching, and he could not spare any thoughts that did not revolve around keeping this city safe.

Cher too came to the top of the wall as did Dawg and the others. Kravin could hear Ta sitting in her usual spot atop one of the wall towers. JP and Skinny were the last two to show up at the wall. At least that was what Kravin had thought once the two men had finally shown up. Katie, however, proved him wrong as she and Lady came to the top of the stairs that led to the spot everyone had gathered in.

"Well, look who it is." Bear looked at Katie as she came walking toward the group. He could not help but notice that something was different about Katie this morning. She had a glow about her and a smile that he had not seen in some time.

Katie moved without saying a word toward Kravin. She and Lady took a spot on either side of the man who would now be leading the forces of the Garden to battle. "Well, I couldn't just leave him to his own devices, could I?" Katie spoke to Bear, her smile was bright and full of joy.

Skinny turned to JP after seeing Katie enter the area, speaking low, hoping no one would hear. "Man, I would love to spend a night with her." His grin full of lust as he eyed Katie; he made no effort to hide what it was he was thinking.

Cher was the one to respond, preventing the conversation to continue any further. "You should probably watch what you say about that particular woman." Her tone was different as well this day. It had a hint of happiness or something Skinny could not really pinpoint. The only thing he did know was that something was different not just about Cher but everyone standing around them.

"Oh yeah, and why is that, sis?" Skinny could not help but be a little sarcastic as he spoke to Cher.

Kravin looked at Skinny as he placed his arm around Katie. He did not say anything to him but instead allowed Katie to do so. "Because I am his wife." Katie pointed to Kravin before giving Kravin a kiss. "Oh, and by the way, my name is Katie. Who are you?"

"This, love, is Skinny and that is JP. They are a bit of a handful, but they are entertaining, and they know how to put up a good fight." Kravin smiled down at his wife as he spoke. Kravin pointed to Skinny and JP as he introduced the two men.

"Well, I guess we will see just how entertaining they are. As for the fighting, I am sure they must be pretty good if Cher trained them." Katie turned to her friend as she said this. Cher stepped forward, returning Katie's look. The two women looked at each other for a moment; they both knew the feelings of the other and respected each other. They had been the best of friends before they had left the city.

Kravin and the others stood in that spot for what seemed like days. They watched the Oritha as they moved closer to the city again. The soldiers had already been alerted and had taken their places outside the walls of the city. Shouting and the clanking of metal filled the air; the machines of war were moved into place, the gears grinding and spitting oil. This would be the greatest battle the Garden had ever seen. Kravin, one of the founding fathers of this great city, would be the conductor of this orchestra as the battle raged.

"Skinny, JP, you two take the same positions you took before. Cher, I want you handling the center. Only this time, we are not leaving any openings in our ranks. You fight with the soldiers. I am sure you can handle giving the orders while ripping these bastards a new one, right?" Kravin smiled at Cher as he spoke to her. He could tell that she was not nervous, nor were any of the others. Everyone who stood on this wall with him had full trust in their friend.

"You know it." Cher turned to leave for her position, running into Skinny and JP as she did so. "What the—? Why are you two still standing here? Move your asses!" Cher shoved both men toward the stairs as she ran past them. Cher had not felt this energized in a long time. It was not because she was eager to finally do battle; no, it was because her family seemed to have come back together if at least for this one moment.

Skinny and JP muttered curses at Cher as the two picked themselves up and began to move to their positions. They two could feel energy in the air that had not been there before. They felt as though they could fight for all eternity. Both men could not help but let their minds wander as they moved. Neither of them had known that Kravin was married or that he had such a stunning wife.

"Ta, if you wouldn't mind, I want you to cover everyone. From here you can see what is happening and can help where it is needed." Kravin looked at the childlike woman as he spoke to her. He was not really sure what she was thinking or how she was feeling. It was obvious to Kravin that there was something bothering her, yet he was not really sure what it was.

"Yeah, I can handle that, babysit everyone else, right?" Her tone was sarcastic as usual. Kravin also noticed that the look that was on her face had changed, replaced with her normal playful expression. It would seem that everything had come together in his favor this day. The only thing left to find out was how the Oritha and their hidden master would react to the plans he had made.

"So, Des, what exactly are you going to do?" Katie looked at Destriga as she spoke to him. It was obvious that she was not being sarcastic but instead she was truly curious as to what this man had planned, given the fact that she had given him his power back.

Destriga panicked for a moment, not really sure how to respond. His face contorted in every way possible before he responded. "Well, to be honest, I figured I would be a last-ditch effort—"

"I would have to agree, Destriga. Katie may have given you a large amount of your power back to you. I am pretty sure that we do not know if you will get it back if you use it again. So you will be our trump card." Kravin looked Destriga directly in the eyes as he spoke to him.

Destriga and Katie both looked at Kravin in surprise as Kravin spoke. Neither of them had fathomed that he would have already known that Destriga had regained his power but also that Katie was the reason for this. "Are you mad?" Katie's voice was low, hoping that her husband would stay calm as he responded to her question.

"Right now, I do not have the luxury of worrying about it. It is done, and there is nothing I can do about it. However, that does not mean we aren't going to talk about this later. You know how I feel about that particular power, and I also know that Des and Bear both know how I feel about them getting you involved in this." Kravin did not show any emotion as he spoke to Katie. He used every ounce of willpower yet again to prevent himself from overreacting to the situation.

"Well, at least you realize that, Kravin." Bear slapped Kravin on the shoulder, supporting his friend and letting him know that he felt he had made the right choice.

Kravin snapped his head toward Bear as he responded to him. His eyes flashed with the energy that coursed through his body. "Do not misunderstand me, brothers, it is all I can do to contain the anger I have for the three of you at this moment. Our conversation will not be one that any of you will enjoy."

Kravin stepped away from his wife, moving closer to the edge of the wall. He stood on the very edge. He looked down on the soldiers that stood below him preparing for the coming battle. He watched on every front as Skinny, JP, and Cher moved to the front of the lines. Once they had taken their positions, he turned his eyes to the sky. It always intrigued him a bit as he was sure it did every great general and commander in history. The calm that came over a battlefield before the chaos and death took over.

Soon many of the men who stood at the gates to this great city would be dead. How many of them would it be was up to Kravin and his friends. He prayed as he looked at this beautiful blue sky that spread out above him and everyone. He prayed that he would have the strength to make the decision he dreaded more than any; if it came down to it.

Kravin finished his prayer and slowly turned his gaze to the horizon. Again, that smoke rose like a pillar taunting him. He had still not figured out why or who was doing all this. However, it did not matter at this time; what did matter was defending this city and crushing the forces that lay before him. Once he had done that, he could find the person who brought such turmoil to his city.

Kravin closed his eyes for a moment, allowing the energy of the day take over. When he opened them, everything about him had changed. He did not stay standing on the wall. Instead he began to float off the wall and move out over the heads of the soldiers that lined the walls below him. He did not look at them. Instead he stared at the Oritha that approached.

"These creatures have come not just to take your lives but the lives of your families and your friends. Resolve yourselves now to fight till your last breath and beyond that. Death will not end your fight. I will not allow that. Those who fall will stand again on this field of battle and give even their afterlife to those who dwell behind these walls. If any of you have any objections, then turn to the man next to you and have him thrust his weapon into your gut. Cowards do not dwell in the Garden of Lost Souls, nor will you taint the blood of other soldiers who give their lives for it." His voice carried the strength of thousands, and his tone made it clear that he was not just trying to inspire the soldiers but giving them an order.

The reaction was a surprise to all of Kravin's friends. The soldiers did not wait or hesitate as they all bellowed words of agreement. None of the men who stood below Kravin feared the words of their commander. Instead, they embraced them and the energy they provided. Every man who fought this day would be the equal of ten. They would all give every last drop of their blood to defend this city, and Kravin was counting on it.

The Oritha that approached the city stopped only a hundred yards from the front lines of the Garden soldiers. They howled and screamed as they stood across the battlefield from their human counterparts. Kravin sneered as he watched them; he had grown to hate these foul creatures over the past few days. The sneer faded and was replaced with an evil grin as he thought about the sight of them being mowed over by the forces of the Garden.

CHAPTER 19

Off in the distance, a sour note was played on some kind of instrument. Kravin watched the Oritha react to this single tone. All at once, the howls and screams ended, replaced by the silence of hate and hunger. Again, the sound pierced through the air, sending chills down the spine of all those who heard it. Kravin again noted a change in the behavior of the Oritha; they had started moving anxiously back and forth. It was this one thing that told him what would happen next.

On the third tone, Kravin bellowed to the men who stood below him. "Hold them HERE!" His eyes flared as the excitement took hold. The Oritha charged across the field toward the soldiers. Unlike before, they did not split their forces. Instead, they spread out evenly across the line. It was obvious that this tactic was as simple as it gets. They had one objective: kill every last soldier that stood between them and the city.

Cher was the first to act of all the soldiers that were on the field. She locked her eyes on the great crescent blade that extended from the end of her halberd. It took only seconds for the blade to glow and shimmer. Cher had trained for years to fight in this way. Her eyes were never on her opponent. Instead, she would stare at the blade of her halberd as she fought. The heat would allow her to cut through any armor; it would sear the flesh of those it hit, sending the smell of burning flesh in the air.

Cher did not just fight with her blade, but she altered the battlefield in her favor. She had never met a creature that could stand the smell of its own burning flesh. She also had never encountered any creature that could stand with her in battle either. This day would be no different than any other.

She reached the first wave of Oritha seconds before any of the Garden soldiers. Cher made a single swipe in front of her, striking down three Oritha at once. She did not think about what she would do next. In truth, given the number of Oritha that were on this battlefield, she knew she could simple swing her halberd in any direction and make contact with one or more of these creatures.

She kept her mind blank from any thought as she danced through the ranks of the Oritha. To see her was to see a ballet play out before one's very eyes as she fought. She relied on her peripheral vision, which is why she needed her mind clear. It allowed her body to react to whatever threat she picked up from the corner of her eyes. It took only a few strikes for the scent of burning Oritha flesh to fill the air. Cher had smelled this particular scent before, and it was almost enough to gag even her. She could do nothing but compare it to spoiled milk left in the sun.

Still though, no matter how strong the scent got, she had to focus on the task at hand. She could not allow this smell to distract her. She danced back and forth, tearing out chunks of the Oritha ranks. The soldiers that fought beside her had been trained not to get within a certain distance of her. They all knew that if they stepped any closer than twenty five feet, that they would be taking their own life with their hands.

Cher had drilled into each of the men that were on this battlefield this day not to get close to her, Skinny, JP, or anyone who stood atop the wall of the city. All the soldiers knew that Bear and Destriga had great abilities when it came to fighting, but none of them had believed Cher at first. It did not, however, take her long to teach them that what she was saying was no idle threat but in fact a reality.

Kravin smiled as he watched the battle unfold before him. His smile grew bigger than it already was as he watched, with hawk-like vision, Cher tore into the ranks of the Oritha. It sent chills of joy down his back seeing the wretched creatures fall before her merciless blade. "You are an entrancing ballerina on the battlefield, my sister. I hope you do not disappoint me."

Kravin turned to view how Skinny had engaged the forces that approached his ranks. His grin grew beyond the proportions of his face at what he could see. The small man moved like a hummingbird through the ranks of the Oritha. Kravin could only compare it to the machine of the past called a heartbeat monitor. Skinny zigged and zagged in and out of the Oritha ranks.

It was obvious to Kravin that Skinny was picking some of his targets with precision. His tactics on the field of battle were the same as his swordplay. He would pinpoint the Oritha that seemed to be giving orders, and when he did, they stood no chance of surviving. His blades flashed like a camera as he moved.

Kravin saw almost every strike the young man made as he fought. He closed his eyes, imaging the scene that was playing out before Skinny. He could see the end of the blades as they cut through flesh and bone alike. He could feel the spray of Oritha blood, warm and sticky. His mind painted a vivid picture of the chaos that was only a few hundred yards away.

It was exactly as Kravin was picturing it in his mind. Skinny moved quickly, staying low to the ground. His blades flashed, finding the vital areas of Oritha, as he moved through the crowd toward his objectives. He was glad that Cher had trained the men to keep their distance from him. He could hear certain Oritha that were not directly on the front line, their voices gruff and low; he did not need to understand their language. Instead, he could tell that they were not yells of battle but instead commands.

That was all he needed to know to mark each of them, making them the target of his strategic strikes. It was simple battlefield logic that even he could understand: remove the officer in charge and the grunts will be lost. He had hoped that by breaking the ranks of the Oritha by killing the commanders, he could save the lives of as many Garden soldiers as he could.

Kravin was delighted at seeing how his friend had learned so much since they had first met. Skinny had always be prone to strike the vital areas of his opponents, but Cher had been the one to hone his skills. She was also the one who had trained him on how to fight a war and not just a battle. Kravin turned to JP, happy that Skinny had been acting according to what Kravin had planned.

The grin that seemed to have expanded the width of Kravin's face did not grow this time. Instead, it shrank a little as he saw what was happening. JP, instead of pushing out into the ranks of the Oritha, was doing all he could to defend from various assaults against him. Kravin thought to himself for a moment, solving the new puzzle that was presented before him.

"It would seem as though they have deemed JP as the weakest link here. Well, I guess it is time for you to show them what you are made of." Kravin turned to Ta, his grin grew as he saw the eager woman stand instantly. "It looks like it is time for you to make your debut." Kravin nodded slightly to the woman before she vanished through one of her portals.

Instantly, Kravin turned to view the ranks of JP's line and his grin was like that of the Cheshire cat. The small woman within seconds had made a drastic difference in the battle. JP, who had been taking blow after blow, was now able to attack back. The daggers that had once hung at Ta's side now covered in blood of the Oritha.

JP stood for a second, watching as Ta attacked; he had never seen this woman fight before and was astounded at the technique she used. Ta did not directly move through the ranks of her attackers. Instead she used her various portals. Striking down one Oritha that stood near her, she would dive, jump, and roll into portals, moving her all over the small area. She would generate portals in front and behind multiple Oritha and would thrust one of her daggers through a portal in front of her. In turn, her hand would thrust the dagger through the neck of each Oritha passing into the portal behind it and striking another.

It took JP a minute or two to get his head back into the fight that was before him. He yelled as he drove back multiple Oritha with his shields. He spun and moved, sidestepping hits, bringing the edge of his shields down on the necks of the Oritha, severing their heads from their bodies, ducking under blows and slamming upward with all his strength, sending Oritha flying backward through the air.

His blood had finally begun to boil as he fought. Thanks to Ta, JP no longer had to defend his position, but instead, he could start pushing back the Oritha that had pinned him down. He screamed with rage and enjoyment as he slaughtered Oritha after Oritha. His brute strength and savagery doing just as much damage to the moral of the Oritha as did his shields to their bodies. None would stand before him without fear; neither Oritha nor Garden soldier would be allowed to do anything less.

Ta returned to her position on the wall, smiling as she licked the blood from her fingers. Kravin smiled at her as she gagged on the foul ooze. "That does not taste as good as I thought it would." She smiled at Kravin, eager to get her next assignment.

Kravin watched as the various lines of his defense pushed the Oritha back. The soldiers of the Garden yelled and screamed as they fought with every ounce of strength they had. They followed Cher, Skinny, and JP as they pushed out away from the city. With those three, the

Garden could give itself some breathing room by keeping the Oritha from the walls.

Now Kravin wondered, *how are you going to react to the fact that I am not coming out and it seems as though my people are more than capable of defending the city and its soldiers?* He stared at the smoke on the horizon; his eyes screamed with malice at the person or persons who were behind this. "So what will you do now?" Kravin bellowed his challenge; every fiber of his being knew that his voice would carry far enough for his opponent to hear him.

It was not a response to his challenge that distracted him at this point. Instead, he caught sight of something he had not imagined. As he watched the center line of his forces, he could see Cher cutting down everything that moved within a certain radius around her. That was not it either, but there was another woman who had moved forward through the ranks of Oritha. She too stood her ground, dismembering and slaughtering any Oritha that came within striking distance of her.

Kravin slowly moved backward toward the wall where Katie and others stood. The grin on his face had disappeared, leaving only a glow of bewilderment. "I didn't know that you had anyone else in the army that was capable of such a feat?" Kravin looked at Bear and Destriga as he spoke. Kravin made it clear that he was slightly insulted by the fact that his two friends had kept this a secret from him.

The two men looked at each other, neither of them sure as to how exactly they should respond to their friend. Katie, however, did not hesitate instead she simply responded to her husband as if it were merely a slip of the mind. "Well she is like her father so I would expect nothing less."

Kravin instantly snapped his head toward his wife. Katie smiled at him knowing that it would not take him more than a second to figure out what it was that she meant. "Are you telling me that is her?" The voice of Kravin did not carry the tone that Katie had expected.

She quickly realized that she had just given him information that may send him over the edge. "Hey, calm down, she is fine, right?" Katie quickly switched gears to keep her husband from doing anything too drastic.

"Fine, what do you mean she is fine?" Kravin pointed out toward the battlefield where the woman was fighting. "She is in the middle of a war! How fine could she be?" His voice seemed almost desperate as he watched the woman.

"She wanted this, Kravin, this is what she has wanted for a long time. To stand with the soldiers of the city and show her father just how strong she is." Katie gripped the arm of Kravin as he began to move outward. Katie knew that if it was up to Kravin he would use all his power to remove the Oritha that were around the woman. "I won't let you take that away from her." Katie's tone was firm as she spoke to her husband; she made it very clear that she would not let Kravin do anything that would ruin this woman's plans.

Kravin stood watching in horror as the woman moved and danced through the field of battle. He knew the blades that she wielded and the style in which fought. It was like seeing a ghost to him. In all the time he had spent alive, he never though he would ever see this woman in this situation. "I can't just let her—"

Katie cut Kravin off before he could finish the statement he had started. "You will not do anything." Her eyes and her tone focused on Kravin as she spoke. It was very clear to Kravin she would stand in his way if he tried anything.

"Fine, I will allow her to continue, but I feel that it is time than I will do something. It will also be the last time she is allowed to set foot on a battlefield." Kravin retorted to his wife with a tone that matched hers. He had given in to her desires, but that did not mean he would abandon his own. "Ta, watch her and do not wait for me to tell you what to do if she gets into any trouble."

"No problem," Ta responded eagerly, her happiness from knowing Kravin had just given her free reign to do whatever she pleased shone through like a light.

As the battle raged between the two forces, it was becoming very obvious that the Garden and its soldiers were not only holding their ground but were also pushing back the Oritha. Yet it seemed as though no matter how many of the Oritha the soldiers of the Garden killed they did not stop coming.

More and more of the Oritha entered the battlefield from some unknown source. Destriga and Bear had both noticed this one fact, yet Kravin did not. He had been caught up in the chaos of the moment. He watched hungrily as Skinny, JP, Cher, and the other woman fought. He no longer cared about anything that was taking place beyond that of the battle that played out right before him.

It appeared to Katie and the others that even though Kravin himself was not fighting in this great battle, he was still being drawn to the battle. It wasn't just that he was being drawn to it, but he was becoming immersed in it. They had to think about what exactly this may cause him to do, and what they may have to do in order to prevent anything too dangerous from happening. It did not take many words though; in reality, it was nothing more than a look between Destriga and Bear that assured what would happen if Kravin were to lose control.

Destriga had been given his strength back for this one possible outcome. Katie could see what was happening to her husband, but she did not fear what he may do. She did not fear that he may lose control either. No, she did not fear anything that was happening with Kravin at this point. Though it was always a little unnerving to see him in this state, she did know that as long as he acted like this, he would be fine.

He had always gotten carried away when watching a battle, and this time was no different. It was something about it that got his blood pumping. Before the flare, it was driving; of course not just driving but driving fast. The speeds that he considered to be cruising speeds were faster than most people had ever driven in their lives. She could not help but smile as she watched her husband let go of everything that was troubling him and indulge himself in one of the few things that really got his energy flowing.

It did not take much time for the energy that Kravin was getting from the battle to stop. The Oritha, realizing that they could not push the forces of the Garden back, in turn began to flee. The battle slowed for now; only a few skirmishes here and there between brave Oritha units and the ranks of the Garden soldiers. Quickly, the officers of the Garden began to assess the situation of their forces and equipment.

Kravin, returning from his frenzy of bloodlust, stood on the wall, watching his troops. He knew how he had acted but made no apologies for it. There was no time for him to be embarrassed about his actions, and to top it off all of those around him had seen him like this before. Instead, he focused his attention on the Oritha that now gathered at the far end of field.

"So, Kravin, what do you think they are going to do now?" Bear was the first to ask Kravin of his opinion.

"We have proven that they can't push us back with pure numbers. We have the strength to repel anything that they throw at us for now. The problem is what they are going to do in order to counter our strength." Kravin analyzed the creatures, hoping to find some kind of hint to what it was that they had planned.

"That answer should be obvious actually. The only way for them to fight our strength is to find strength of their own." Destriga was the only one who was willing to point this simple fact out.

"Yeah, I just wonder if the strength that will come forth is the same strength that is trying to bring me out." Kravin could not help but shudder slightly at the thought of what may be coming. He had been focusing on it for so long, yet he still could not imagine who or what it was that was trying to bring him out to fight. It did not matter though, he had seen what his people were capable of and it was more than enough to keep him from fighting.

Destriga and Bear too joined Kravin as he stared at their enemy across the field. They were all very curious as to who it was that had tried to bully Kravin in to a confrontation. It was actually kind of comical to Destriga and Bear both that someone actually thought they could get him to fight in the way they had chosen. Everyone who knew Kravin knew that there was one thing that he would not allow happen.

Destriga and Bear were one of the few people who knew why Kravin had left the city so long ago. They knew just how terrified Kravin was of his own power. It was something that would keep him up for extended amounts of time. No, Kravin would never allow someone to push him to the point that he would risk losing control just to make a point.

Destriga knew that was all this was the attack on the Garden and the curse placed on him and Bear. It was all an attempt by someone to try and bully Kravin into using his power. No not just using his power but using enough that would cause him to lose control of it and doing something he would regret. Someone out there wanted Kravin to destroy the things he held dear, and they were putting a lot of effort into it.

Bear could not help but look at Kravin and wish he could do something to help the man he called his brother. He knew that this man who stood calm and collected before him in truth held a great burden. He had taken on the task of protecting this city, and it turned out to be exactly what their enemy had wanted. Neither Destriga nor Bear had any idea that this was the strategy or objective of the person they were fighting.

Instead they were too caught up in the fact that they could not recuperate their power and their soldiers did not have the skills or equipment to really stop the Oritha. Their numbers were also too small for them to really push them back either. They could not begin to think of anything except for finding help for the city they held dear. Yet how could someone have known that they would turn to Kravin for help and he would in fact try and help them? It all seemed so important, yet it also seemed to be irrelevant at this time as well.

CHAPTER 20

Though the Oritha had pulled back for now, it did not matter to Kravin or the others. It also looked as though it did not matter to the soldiers as well. All the soldiers who stood outside the city stood guard, waiting to see if the Oritha would come again this day. They prepared for what they all felt would be the inevitable. The Oritha would come again, but this time, they would not attack as they did before.

Kravin had assumed that this may happen if they managed to shut down the attack of the Oritha. It was something that to him seemed the most logical thing for his opponent to do. They needed to learn what he would do in an all-out attack. Now they had the information they wanted; this time they would not just mindlessly throw everything they had at him. This time they would do something to try and break the line of the Garden.

The only problem that Kravin could see was that he had no idea as to what his opponent would do in order to achieve this. Do they have some kind of advanced war machines that could decimate the Garden soldiers? Perhaps there was some kind of magic they had been keeping to themselves until now. Everything at this point would have to rely on the decisions of Bear and Destriga.

"Bear, Destriga, I have to tell you that I have no idea as to what is going to happen now. I have planned up until now. You two were the ones who were able to react to changing situations, not me." Kravin knew the limits of his abilities when it came to strategy. No matter how hard he tried to plan for every possible outcome, there were always things that he could not account for. This time, however, he had accounted for one thing, that he did not have enough information to plan out everything that would happen in this battle.

"Well it's about time you gave up the spotlight." Destriga stepped forward, looking off into the distance at the opponent that was preparing for their next assault. His chipper attitude reflected the energy he had been able to recover, thanks to Katie.

Bear, however, did not move as quickly as Destriga, his energy still lacking. Kravin could tell that his friend was straining to see as he had before. Bear had always been known for his amazing eyesight. Not for how far he could see but what he would notice. He had always been able to pick out the smallest details which in turn Destriga and Kravin could react and make changes to plans because of those details.

Kravin could not help but think about how this battle would go given the state of Bear. Yet he could not bring himself to ask Katie to give up her life force in order to help Bear. He could not bear to think that she would be shortening her own life span. He would have to do as much as he could to help Bear notice the things that needed to be noticed. "Ta, I want you moving among all the commanding officers down there if the Oritha return. We are going to need as much information we can get."

"What? You mean I have to be a messenger if they come back? What happen to helping wherever it is needed?" Ta did not hesitate to display her disdain of no longer being able to fight and instead taking on a supporting role.

"I realize you like killing quite a bit, Ta, but I need you doing this more than I need you killing." Kravin returned Ta's snippy attitude with one of his own. One that allowed for no arguments.

"Fine, but don't get mad at me if something happens and the Oritha breaks through." Ta turned away from

Kravin, whipping her hair, using it as another indicator
that she was not satisfied with the job she had been given.

Katie tugged at the arm of Kravin, trying to get his
attention. She had seen the same thing in Bear that
Kravin had. She knew that Bear would not be as useful as
he would be if he had his energy. "We need to talk."
Katie motioned to Kravin as she began to walk away from
everyone. Kravin followed his wife knowing that it must
be important; otherwise, she would not have bothered to
say anything at this particular time.

"What is it?" Kravin had feared what it was that Katie
would say once they had gotten far enough away from
everyone. He had already gone over multiple things that
she could say to him at this point and there was only one
thing that he hoped was not it.

"Let me help Bear. You and I both know that he would
be much more help if I did." The tone in Katie's voice was
very serious. She cared for this city and the people who
lived in it just as much as Kravin. Which was why she was
willing to use her costly power to help defend it.

This was what Kravin had feared she would say. He
knew how she felt about the city, but at the same time
how could he let her use a power like that? It took him
what seemed like hours before he finally responded to his
wife. "If things start going badly during the battle, then
and only then will I agree to you using your power on

Bear." This was all he could do to try and keep Katie happy and safe at the same time.

Katie looked at Kravin for a moment after hearing is decision. She knew that it was not a good time for her to try and argue with him. Yet at the same time she felt that he was putting the city in danger for not allowing her to help Bear. She stood looking at her husband, a look of helplessness on her face as Kravin turned away from her.

After finishing his discussion with Katie, Kravin returned to his friends in order to begin preparing for what might happen next. The three men deliberated over many strategies and possibilities of what may come. The minutes went by; each of the three men watched the horizon for some sign of their enemy. It was not until a few hours later that they finally saw something on the horizon. At first it appeared as though they had figured out what the strategy of their opponent was. It became very clear that they were wrong.

At first, the Oritha had all gathered together as they marched forward to the walls of the Garden and the soldiers that stood beneath them. As Kravin and the others watched, the ranks of the Oritha parted. The Oritha army did not come across the field this time, instead it stopped dead after reaching the halfway point. Seconds after the Oritha forces stopped moving, the ground itself began to shake. Not like the movement of an army or of any large war machines. These were things that the forces of the Garden were used to. This, however, was something different.

There were no loud noises that accompanied the shaking. Slowly, though, the shaking became stronger and stronger. Soon Kravin began to hear the source of the quakes. He could just barely make it out; it was some kind of clanking. Kravin did not really understand what was going on until he saw the source of the sound begin moving forward through the parted ranks of Oritha.

The man was by no means small, standing at what Kravin assumed to be around nine or ten feet tall. Kravin was not sure if he really was human or something else. What he did know was that this thing was covered in armor from head to toe. It moved slowly, lumbering from side to side as it walked. The clanking of its armor plates resonating through the air. It took a few seconds before Kravin heard the gasps of his friends, letting him know that they two had seen what the source of the quaking is.

"My god." Katie said nothing more as she squeezed the arm of Kravin. Kravin understood why his wife would be nervous about this seemingly mound of moving metal. He himself was not sure if anyone on their side could do anything to stop it.

"That it one huge son of a bitch." Bear stared in awe at the figure that stood across the field of battle from him. Quickly his thoughts changed from awe to anger. Anger at the fact that he could not fight him himself. He knew that in his weakened condition, he would be no match for this thing. He stole a glance at Katie, his thoughts selfish.

"Well, I wonder what he plans on doing." Destriga was calm as he watched the creature standing on the battlefield. He analyzed every movement of the Oritha forces and the man. All his concentration was simply finding a way to win this war.

"What do you think we should do?" Katie looked to her husband, hoping that he would have some kind of plan to stop not just the Oritha but the metal-covered creature that now stood at the head of them.

"Well, since he came all this way, I guess we should go and see what it is that he wants." Kravin turned to Bear and Destriga, looking to see if his two friends agreed with his chosen course of action.

"I assume that is what he is expecting me or us to do. So what the hell . . . let's do it." Destriga grinned at Kravin as he agreed. It was obvious he was just as interested in the armored figured as Kravin was.

"Hell yeah, I say we just go kick his ass and call it a night." Bear moved toward the edge of the wall. His speed almost carrying him over the edge. Kravin and Bear both smiled seeing how energetic their friend had become at the sight of what he perceived as a worthy opponent.

"Calm down, Bear, I wasn't exactly planning on all of us going out there. I figured we would let Cher and the soldiers handle it for now. We will enjoy the show and help if it is necessary. Besides, you are in no condition to fight." Kravin clasped the shoulder of his friend, helping to relay the message that he was not going to fight.

Bear turned to face Kravin, his eyes looking around Kravin for just a second, stealing yet another look at Katie. Kravin, however, did not choose to ignore this particular hope of Bear's. "My wife may be able to help you, Bear, but she will not do so just so you can go have fun wasting the energy she gives you. It will only happen if it is an emergency. Do you understand me?" Kravin looked Bear in the eye as he said this. There would be no mistake that Kravin would not allow any waste of the power Katie could provide Destriga and Bear.

"Fine, I get it, but don't go thinking that I won't go after that guy if I get my powers back. If he isn't dead when I get my powers back, then he will be after I get ahold of him." Bear smiled evilly as he agreed to Kravin's demands.

Kravin turned from his friend, accepting the deal Bear had made. "Ta, let Cher know that it is time for the Garden to meet their challenge. She should be able to make the correct decision as to how many men she should leave behind, and, Ta, don't come back here. You stay with Cher." Kravin smiled at the tiny woman as she eagerly jumped through one of her portals. "Now then, we get to see just what it is they have up their sleeve."

Kravin turned to face the Oritha and the metal-covered creature.

Kravin stood as Cher led the majority of the Garden soldiers toward the center of the field. Again, the silence that came before the storm fell on the field of battle. The soldiers of the Garden, inspired by their previous victory, walked with confidence. The Oritha who would normally be roaring and pounding the ground instead stayed silent. This metal figure that stood at the head of the Oritha somehow changed their demeanor.

Cher eyed the large creature as she too moved across the battlefield. She cannot see any real weak points in the creature's armor. Every square inch of it seemed to be covered by metal plating. She could see the difference in the Oritha forces as well, but she could not help but feel something was off. She looked back and forth, scanning the lines of the Oritha, looking for anything that came as a surprise to them. Still, it seemed that the only thing that had changed was this hulk of metal that stood out front.

"So, sis, how fun do you think that one is going to be?" Ta was the only one in the forces of the Garden that spoke, her smile wider than it had been in a long time.

"I am not sure just how fun it will be, but I do know that he is not going down without a fight." Cher cannot help but be slightly amused by how voracious this small woman was when it came to fighting.

Ta didn't look at Cher but instead stared hungrily at the creature. Her hands twitched at the thought of fighting this monstrosity. Her steps hastened as the two forces came closer and closer together. There was little she could do to control her excitement as she looked at her chosen opponent. She would not allow anyone to come between her and her prey.

Cher tried not to encourage the small woman who seemed to be leading the pace of the soldiers. She did not want to engage the Oritha without getting a full understanding as to what was going to happen. So the only way to do that was to keep Ta on a short leash, which Kravin seemed to be the only person capable of doing so. Finally, Cher felt that it was necessary to stop Ta. "Ta, stop. We aren't ready to engage yet."

Ta looked back at Cher for a second, her expression twisted with confusion. Her anticipation of the coming battle blinding her to Cher's order. It wasn't until a booming voice seemed to clear away every thought she had. *"That is far enough, Ta."* Ta, knowing that Kravin would not tolerate her ignoring him, finally stopped moving forward.

"Thanks." Cher stepped next to Ta, looking down at the small woman as she did, appreciating that fact that Ta had stopped moving forward.

"Don't thank me. The only reason I stopped was because he said so." Ta frowned as she told Cher the reason she had stopped moving.

Cher could not help but think how thankful she was that Kravin had been paying attention to what Ta was doing. Of course Cher also knew that Kravin knew enough about Ta that he would not have told her to stay here if he had not planned to watch her. Either way, Cher could not help but feel grateful for it.

The metal creature was close enough for Cher to make out details now. The armor that shone so brightly across the battlefield seemed almost impenetrable from here. It was obvious that many hours were spent polishing the armor in order to give such a brilliant shine. Dents and dings throughout it suggested that there may have been many scratches on the armor, all of which had been removed.

Cher could make out two eyes just inside the helmet; yet the face was locked in darkness. Cher could not tell if the eyes were glowing red, which caused the darkness, or if the helmet was just that large. Whatever the case, the creature did not seem to be encumbered by the amount of armor. The creature returned the look of Cher; a small sigh seemed to emanate from the creature.

The creature did not say anything to Cher or the Garden soldiers. It simply raised the huge axe it had carried to the battlefield high above its head with one arm. Cher could not help but feel a little awe-inspired at seeing the strength the creature possessed. The axe was larger than any man in the army of the Garden; it would also cleave through any of them with little effort.

It took Ta nudging Cher to pull her out of her thoughts. Cher had been standing there, watching the creature, but did not recognize the fact that it was beginning to signal a charge. "Thanks." Cher quickly readied her halberd as she thanked Ta.

The two women readied themselves, sending the signal to the rest of the Garden soldiers that they too needed to ready themselves. Both women stared at the monstrous creature that stood holding its giant axe in the air. Neither of them had sweat as much as they did at this very moment—Cher because she was not sure just how things were going to happen, Ta on the other hand from anxiety over being able to fight someone who may prove to be a challenge. What happened next was a surprise to both of them.

The creature raised his foot in the air, leaning backwards as he did this. His axe never wavered, staying straight as an arrow. It held this pose for a second before finally bringing its foot down. The head of the axe swung forward, smashing the ground. At the same second the axe hit the ground, hundreds of Oritha leapt from behind the front lines. They flew high over Ta and Cher, landing beyond the front lines of the Garden soldiers.

The axe of the large creature split the ground beneath it. A crevice formed, spreading out, swallowing those Garden soldiers who did not react quick enough to get away. Cher watched as her men lost their lives without even having a chance to fight. Quickly, she turned back to the creature that had caused the crevice. To her surprise, it did not move forward. Instead, it simply hefted its axe over its shoulder and waited.

Ta, seeing the Oritha leap and the crevice that had formed, reacted without hesitation. She did not care about the soldiers that were around her. The only thing that she cared about was getting to the creature and testing its might. Ta opened a portal that lead just behind the creature and moved to step through. Just before she had completely vanished, she caught a look of the creature who seemed to be looking right at her as she moved.

She had only a second to react as she came out of the other side of the portal. The large axe's head came within a fraction of an inch of her face as she fell backward. Somehow, the creature had known what it was Ta was going to do. She lay staring up at the monster that stood before her. Being this close to it gave her a whole new understanding of just how daunting a foe it was. She stood no higher than its hips; the head of the axe it carried was even taller than she.

It did not matter though; she would kill this thing no matter what. Instantly, she created a portal below her, falling into it. This time she had targeted the area above the creature, hoping to catch it off guard as she fell on top of it. This time, however, the axe did not miss its mark. As Ta came out of her portal, she fell directly on the blunt head of the axe. The creature, feeling her weight on its weapon, looked toward Cher and tossed the small woman toward her.

"You?" came a shrill voice from the armor. Obviously mocking both Ta and Cher.

Cher managed to catch Ta without being knocked over. "Are you OK?"

"Yeah, I am fine, but somehow this son of a bitch knew where I was coming from." The face of Ta showed nothing but anger as she stood on her own. Instantly, she gripped her daggers even tighter than she had before, preparing for another attack against the creature. Just as she was about to generate her portal, she was interrupted.

"We got this, sista. Kravin said we need to help you guys out. So stand back and watch a man work." Skinny jumped in front of Ta, blocking her view of the creature.

"WHAT!" Ta's voice shrieked at the two men who had just taken her prey from her. *Of all the time for these two idiots to get in the way. To top it off, Kravin gave them a pass*; these were the thoughts that raged in the mind of Ta as she watched the two men engage the monster.

JP instantly moved toward the monster, hoping to block its view of Skinny who stayed in the large man's shadow. JP ignored the fact that he came only to the shoulders of the monster. He had fought many men who were bigger than him, but never by this much. It did not matter to him though; Cher had trained both of them for so long no one could withstand their attacks.

The axe of the creature came crashing down towards JP; instantly, JP, using both of his arms, blocked the attack. His eyes went wide as the force of the blow drove him to his knees. He had used both of his arms to stop the axe, yet the force was beyond anything he had ever felt. He could do nothing but stare at the red glow that emanated from the helmet of the monster.

His stunned mind was pulled back to reality as Skinny leaped off his shoulders, striking a blow at the helmet of the monster. Both men now expressed shock as the monster, clad in armor, had the reflexes to move its head, deflecting the strike from the short sword of Skinny off the side of its great helmet. Instantly, the creature hooked the arms of JP with the head of the axe, yanking him forward, while slamming the axe handle into the abdomen of Skinny.

The creature knew the strategy of the two men and did exactly what it needed in order to prevent them from using it. Without hesitation, both JP and Skinny began attacking the creature. JP, knowing he could not do anything with the edges of his shields against the creature's armors, opted for his fists. It proved to be just as effective as the shields. The creature never once tried to block any of the blows from JP, instead allowing the man to strike it.

Instead, it parried the strikes of Skinny and attacked JP. The three fought for minutes in this fashion; none of them yielding to the other. Somehow, JP and Skinny had managed to work their way closer together, again hoping to use their strategy, though both men had decided they would need to try something a little different if they were to beat this creature. It was something they had tried only once against Cher, who proved to be too quick for the maneuver. They hoped that this creature was not as quick.

Instead of JP attacking the creature first, it was Skinny who initiated the attack. His blade moved quickly as he pushed towards the creature. His speed kept the axe inches from making contact; he did not care if he actually hit, but instead he simply wanted to keep the pressure on the creature. JP was the one who was supposed to make the final blow.

Skinny ducked as the creature brought the great axe over its head. Broadcasting a blow from above, instantly, Skinny sidestepped, seeing an opening in the abdomen of the creature. His swords instantly lashed out at the area where the kidneys would be. His eyes grew wide, and his jaw dropped as both of his swords simply clanked off the armor of the creature.

The creature in turn cackled as it brought the head of the axe down toward Skinny. JP, however, intercepted the blow, gripping the axe just above the hands of the creature. "I don't think so." JP forced out the words as he strained to hold back the axe. It was obvious to JP that this creature was much stronger than he was. It did not matter though; Cher had taught him many things, and handling larger opponents was one of them.

Instantly, he twisted his body, shoving his butt into the hip of the creature. Pulling with all his might, he yanked the axe forward and down. Surprised, JP found himself looking down at the face of the creature he had just tossed over his hip. Cher had told him how it to do it, yet he never though it would actually work. The creature too, surprised by what had just happened, loosened its grip on the axe long enough for JP to rip it from its hands.

The axe, though heavy to JP, did not seem as though it was un-wieldable. JP gripped the axe in the most comfortable way he could manage, giving it a few quick swings, testing just how proficiently he could wield it. He knew that if Skinny or he had any chance of defeating the creature, it was now. Both men looked at the creature as it stood, spreading its arms, taunting the two men.

CHAPTER 21

JP and Skinny readied themselves for the start of round two with this metal monster. Neither of them were very sure as to what they should do or how they should do it. The only thing they agreed on was that they will both go all-out to defeat this creature. Making this decision, the two men began to circle the creature, Skinny holding both of his swords and JP now wielding the axe stolen from the creature. The three moved in what seemed like an endless circle, waiting for the chance to strike.

JP was the first to make his attack. He moved slower than Skinny, especially wielding this giant axe. He rushed the creature, stopping just within striking distance of his newly acquired axe. He launched a huge swing with the axe, aiming for the legs of the creature, hoping to hook one so that he make take him down. A moment of shock passed over him as he achieved his goal. It was quickly overtaken by terror as the creature merely looked at him, knowing JP did not have the strength to pull the creature from his feet.

Skinny, reacting to the movements of JP, dashed forward, knowing his friend would try to knock the creature down. At first he was planning to simply leap up and drive his swords through the sockets in the helmet of the creature. Instead he quickly changed his tactic, seeing that JP could not bring the creature to the ground. Instead, he jumped on the creature's back, digging, clawing for some weak point in the creature's armor. What he found was nothing.

Realizing this, Skinny quickly realized the creature's eyes were open and that he could strike within the helmet as he had planned before. Latching himself to the back of the creature with his legs, he quickly lined up his attack, hoping to strike a fatal blow before things got any worst for JP and him. It was too late though; the creature grabbed each blade inches before Skinny plunging them into its eyes.

Skinny was sure the creature giggled slightly as it twisted, throwing Skinny of its back in the crowd that surrounded the three. At the same time, it yanked the foot JP had hooked with his axe. The strength of this awed JP as he too went flying into the crowd around them. It took both men a second to realize what had just happened to them. The brute force of this creature was far greater than any they had ever seen before. It did not matter though; the two men would not give up. Instantly, they jumped to their feet and again readied themselves for a fight.

Instead though, they found Cher squaring off with the creature. Her eyes glowed the brightest red the two had ever seen. The blade of her halberd matching the glow with its own. Cher looked calm as she looked at the creature who had just trounced her two disciples. Skinny and JP both could not help but feel slightly disappointed as they watched Cher, both knowing that their opportunity to take down this behemoth was over.

Cher looked at the creature, analyzing the movements it had just made. She went over and over again how the creature behaved and fought. At first it seemed as though it was just quick, relying on it reflexes to counter both the boys' and Ta's attacks. Now, though, it was very obvious; whatever this thing was, it was thinking, and it knew that neither JP nor Skinny had the ability to take it down.

"Well, you big son of a bitch, you might be able to beat them, but how about some hot steel to warm you up?" Cher mumbled under her breath before readying herself to attack the creature. Again, the monster that stood across from her did nothing. It simply stared at her as if waiting for an attack it felt was futile. Cher did not rush the creature. Instead, she chose to move slowly toward it, seeing how it would react to this style of combat.

She had gotten about halfway to her opponent when the creature moved. One huge step was all it took, shaking the ground beneath it. Soldiers and Oritha caught off guard were knocked to the ground, allowing their opponents to strike killing blows. The screams of men and Oritha alike sounded like a chorus around Cher. Everything all at once hit a chord somewhere in Cher's subconscious, freezing her in place. She knew that she could not afford it, but she no longer had control of her own body.

The creature, seeing Cher paralyzed by the shock of everything, did nothing but point. Its large armored hand raised a pointing finger at Cher, as if telling her that the next scream would be from her. The creature never said a word or made any noise during this whole time, allowing its overgrown body to do all the talking that was needed.

She must win this fight. She has to take down this giant tin can; otherwise, the battle will be lost. This was the thought that overpowered Cher's mind as she finally regained her composure. It seemed that trying to take the battle slowly would not be a good idea. She would have to keep the fighting going as much as possible until she could find the opening she needed in order to take this creature down.

Cher let her guard down for a moment, looking at the creature. She simply stood with her halberd at her side, analyzing the creature. This of course was a tactic, though one that could be very costly. She had hoped that if she treated this creature as if it were nothing more than any other soldier, that perhaps she could convince it to make some mistake. Though the reaction she did get was not what she expected.

"Well, well, aren't we a little cocky, miss? To think that someone who a moment ago looked as if they had just pissed their panties would take such a nonchalant stance before me." The voice of the creature hissed from the armor.

"Well, to be honest, I was shocked at how pathetic you really are. Cheap tricks to try and scare me, is that the best you can do?" Cher used all the will she could muster to make her words sounds as convincing as possible.

"Cheap tricks!" A shrill laugh erupted from the armor, sounding as if it were echoing from within. "What cheap tricks are you talking about, lass? I simply knocked a hundred men and Oritha over so that they could merely set the mood. You can't dance without a good melody, you know."

"Dance? Is that what this is to you?" Cher could not help but let her temper come forth as the creature described the battle to her.

"Why yes. A dance is all this really is, lass. Do you know the best part though?" The creature bent forward slightly as if trying to get on the same level as Cher.

"What?" Cher did not care what the creature had to say at this point. Instead of waiting for it to respond, she instead jumped at the creature, twirling her blade, hoping to strike its helmet. The creature reacted quicker than she had expected though, stepping out of the way. Cher quickly stopped her forward movement, turning on the hilt of the halberd, landing a kick to the head of the creature. Though she swore the pain for her was far greater than the pain the creature probably felt.

It didn't matter though; she had felt much greater pain than this before. She would not let this stop her or hinder her ability to fight. She concentrated for a moment, willing the pain to stop. She knew that in order for her to land a blow, she had to move faster with her halberd. The only way to do that was to lose the things that were slowing her movements. She had planned for situations like this, pulling one of the straps that held the bodice of her armor.

She needed to wiggle slightly in order to get the armor to fall from her chest. It was one of the few times she wished she was not so well endowed in that particular region. It didn't matter though; without that piece of armor, she had lost thirty pounds and restriction to her movement. She had not realized just how cool the breeze was that was blowing across the field. The cotton which her shirt was made from did little to stop the air.

The air cooled her soft skin, giving her a sense of revitalization. It was not until this moment that she had realized she was slightly tired. The Oritha were not much of a challenge, so she had not noticed how much energy she had spent during the battle. It was quickly becoming evident to her that this was one of the main reasons that the soldiers had been able to push out this far. It was also coming very apparent that she should not have pushed so hard and allowed the soldiers to do more work.

All this was relevant though now. She had to focus on fighting this creature and slaying it. It was the only hope not just for the soldiers and to win the battle but also the only hope the Garden had of surviving. Cher finally shook all the clutter from her head, eliminating the useless thoughts that had been running through her mind. It was time for her to end this battle right here and now.

Cher dove forward, thrusting the halberd out towards the creature. In turn, the creature turned and stepped backward with its right foot, evading the strike. Quickly, Cher turned the blade of her halberd sideways; pivoting on her heel, she put all her weight behind the shaft of the halberd. The creature, seeing this, spun to its left again, evading her attack. Pushing off its back foot, the creature lunged forward at Cher with its fist.

Cher ducked, spinning completely around, hoping to catch the leg of the creature with the blade of her halberd. The creature, leaping over her blade, came down with both fist. Cher shoved the hilt of her halberd into the dirt, pushing with her legs, flipping out of the way as the creature landed. The force of the creature's blow left a crater in the ground. Quickly, Cher spun her halberd around her waist, pushing the creature back.

After missing the second time, she thrust the halberd forward, hoping to stab the creature. Instead, the creature stepped sideways, grabbing the shaft of her halberd. Quickly, Cher jumped, gripping the hilt of the halberd as tightly as possible, stepping off the side of the head of the creature as it grabbed for her. The full weight of Cher would be on the wrist of the creature. She had hoped to break its wrist by doing this.

The creature, realizing Cher's goal, quickly released the shaft of her halberd. Cher landed in time to cover her abdomen as the foot of the creature struck her. Pushing her back, the creature went on the offensive, seeing that it had slightly knocked the wind from Cher. She moved the blade of the halberd, deflecting one fist, the other connecting with her abdomen once again.

The blow was almost as heavy as the one from the creature's foot. The creature grabbed for Cher's head; reacting, she quickly dropped and rolled backwards, avoiding the grapple. The foot of the creature blotted out the sun as it came down over Cher. Cher rolled again and again as the creature simply tried to step on her. The last time Cher rolled, she felt the huge hand grip her hair. She knew that it had only missed her head by inches.

She had little time to react as she was flung in the air; pain shot through her scalp as the creature tore hair from her head. Cher managed to balance herself in the air as she came back down. Aiming, she brought the halberd down over her head as she landed. The creature dove to its left, evading the blow. Cher rolled to her right, thrusting the halberd out toward the creature as she stood.

Her aim was off just a little, affected by the pain that was throbbing through her scalp. Still, she saw sparks fly from the armor of the creature as the blade grazed off its hip. The creature groaned slightly as Cher pulled the blade back toward her, blocking the fist of the creature. Again and again, the fists of the creature landed heavily on the shaft of the halberd.

The creature's blows were starting to take their toll on Cher legs. She knew that she could not allow this creature to pound on her as it was. Cher parried the last blow; she brought the blade of her halberd down on the creatures arm. A growl came from somewhere inside the armor of the creature as the blade ripped through its forearm. Gripping the shaft tightly, the creature flung Cher toward the crowd that surrounded them. Cher balanced herself in the air, landing on her feet, slamming the hilt of her halberd into the ground as a brake.

"Well, I have to admit, lass, you have been doing surprisingly well. I had no idea that there was anyone within the walls of that city aside from Bear or Destriga who might pose as a challenge to me." The creature stood, facing Cher again, its posture as if she was nothing.

"What do you know of Destriga and Bear?" Cher allowed her emotions to flare as she spoke to the creature.

"Oh, I know quite a bit, lass. Destriga the great mage, he who can rip the heavens from the very sky. Bear the brute with endless strength, the man who can move the earth itself. Oh, and lest we forget the fallen one. Kravin." The creature hissed the name of Kravin as if taunting Cher.

Instantly hearing the creature speak the name of Kravin, Cher lunged once again at the creature. She brought the blade of the halberd down over head. The creature side stepped backwards, avoiding the blade by less than an inch. Cher stopped her strike mid-swing. Instead, she thrust the blade of her halberd forward again. The creature merely stepped slightly to its left, raising its arm, allowing the strike to pass underneath.

"Come now, don't be like that, lass. Kravin isn't what everyone thinks he is. Though I am pretty sure very few within those walls remember him anymore. Though it would seem you do, but you aren't from those walls, are you?" The creature stepped to his side, barely avoiding yet another strike from Cher.

"What do you want with him?" Cher yelled as her angered boiled over. Her swings, once graceful, now desperate to slay the creature before her.

"Well, I know he has power beyond anything this world has seen. A power capable of destroying everything it touches. Power he himself is unable to control. A power that does not belong to him." The creature leaped backwards from Cher, narrowly avoiding yet another strike from her.

Confusion blanketed the mind of Cher as she heard those words from the creature. What did he mean by power that is not his? How did he know that Kravin left the city? Not only that but how did he know that she was with him? What is all this about, and how does this creature know so much about Kravin? "Who are you?"

Cher lashed out at the creature, blow after blow, missing her marks as she attacked. The creature grunted and groaned as it stepped sideways and backward, evading each blow. "Who am I?" The creature ducked as Cher tried to strike its head. "I, dear lass." Again, the creature stopped talking for a moment, evading a blow from Cher's halberd. "Am the one leading this dance." The creature grabbed the blade of Cher's halberd this time.

Panic crossed the face of Cher as she realized what had happened. The creature had played her this whole time. It had distracted her as they were fighting. It had known that as long as Cher was looking at her blade, she could cut through its armor with ease. Now though the blade was nothing but cold steel, and she was in trouble.

The creature jerked the halberd forward, pulling Cher to it. The creature grasped Cher around the waist with one metal hand. "Be a dear and tell Kravin I need a new dance partner, lass." The creature tossed Cher in the air after saying this. Cher, still in awe from her situation, did not react in time to evade the blow. The creature, wielding her halberd as a bat swung, connecting to Cher's rib cage, sending her flying toward the walls of the Garden.

She could not believe the strength of the creature. She heard each of her ribs break as the hilt of her halberd connected. She felt the air blowing through her hair as she flew through the air. It took only a second before her sight went black. When she awoke, she was lying on the ground at the feet of Ta, who stood in shock at what had just happened to Cher.

"Yeah, so you just got knocked the—" Ta grinned at Cher as she spoke.

"Yeah, I know, don't rub it in." Cher quickly moved to stand, but her broken ribs sent pain shooting through her body, preventing her from moving.

Craig E. Hays

CHAPTER 22

JP and Skinny had been standing around watching the fight between Cher and the armored creature. They watched as they fought the Oritha that might interrupt the battle between the two. Neither of the men expected to see Cher be dominated in a fight like this. Both of them were shocked as they watched the woman who had trained them be sent flying through the air, hit like a baseball with her own weapon.

The two men shared a look as anger took over. They would get revenge on this monster for doing what it had just done to Cher. They would rip it limb from limb; there was no way that they could lose. This creature would not get away with treating Cher like a mere toy. The two readied their weapons and prepared to charge this creature once again.

The creature looked at both men as they entered the circle that had formed around it. A deep chuckle erupted from its armor. "You two again? Didn't you learn the first time that you don't have a prayer of beating me?"

"Yeah well, we didn't take you all that serious the first time, so now get ready for a beating." Skinny moved side to side like a snake ready to strike. He did not need to talk to JP; the two had spent so much time fighting together they knew the movements of each other.

JP gripped the handle of the axe tightly as a thought came to his mind. Skinny and he could barely make Cher work hard during training, and this creature treated her as if she was an amateur. How could the two of them hope to do what Cher couldn't even do? It didn't matter though; they would take this creature down for Cher.

JP was the first to attack, jumping forward at the creature, swinging the huge axe overhead. The creature in turn went to step to the side, finding Skinny, their swords clashing against its armor. The creature deflected two blows with its armored hands as JP came down. The force of the blow from JP sent dust flying into the air, shrouding the three fighters for a moment. As the dust settled and the three could be seen again, the blow from JP did not connect. Instead it was stopped by the hands of the creature.

It had grabbed the blade on either side with each hand. "Not good enough, lad." The creature turned the blade, spinning JP in the air. Stepping and bringing the handle of the axe toward the ground, the creature smashed JP into the ground. Still holding the blade of the axe, the creature spun; JP, who had let go of the axe, was stunned on the ground. As the creature spun, the handle of the axe connected with Skinny as he leaped to strike the creature. The blow sent Skinny tumbling across the ground.

JP jumped to his feet and waited for Skinny to recover from the attack. His thoughts raced as he waited, keeping his distance from the creature. How could the two of them be shut down by this creature so easily? He had strength and mass to stop the blows, and Skinny had the speed and precision. Yet this one creature seemed to poses more than both of them combined.

Skinny walked forward after he recovered from the blow he had just taken. Luckily, he had managed to move his swords in time to block the blow; otherwise, he would have been taken out of the fight. No thoughts crossed his mind except beating this creature. They would get revenge for Cher, and there was no way this creature would beat them. Skinny spun his swords so the blade now faced backward.

Skinny glanced to JP, signaling him that he was going to attack. Skinny charged the creature, sidestepping as the axe handle thrust out toward him. He ducked and moved under the handle to the side of the creature. He landed three blows to the abdomen of it. Each of which were met with a loud tang of steel on steel. None of them penetrated the massive armor of this creature.

JP, seeing Skinny attack, charged the creature as well. Instead of trying to make a blow, he instead chose to grab the leg of the creature, stopping it from moving. Hearing the blows of Skinny deflect of the creature's armor, his anger flared. Instantly, he began to lift up on the leg of the creature. Farther and farther he lifted; the creature, realizing what was happening, turned its attention from Skinny to JP.

It landed four heavy blows, each ending with a heavy thud on the body of JP. It was too late, however. JP had already affected the balance of the creature. JP, feeling that he had gained control over the creature's balance, lifted with all his might, sending the creature falling to its back. Letting go of the creature's leg, he began to push as the creature lay on its back. If he could break its leg, maybe they would have a chance.

Skinny, seeing the creature lying on its back, saw his opportunity to attack the one area that did not have armor. He leaped on to the chest of the creature, pointing his swords at the eyeholes of the creature's helmet. Before he could land his blows though, the creature grabbed him, tossing him into JP, knocking both of them backward. They had come so close, yet one mistake had caused them to fail. It was a mistake they would not make again.

Both men stood, understanding the objective they now had. JP, allowing his rage to take control, charged the creature once again. This time instead of going for the creature's leg, he instead grabbed the creature around the waist. The creature howled as he realized what the man was trying to do. JP gripped the creature with all his might and began to lift.

Skinny circled around the creature, getting behind it. Seeing the creature begin to strike JP, he began to attack the arms of the creature. He had taken on the role of JP and was deflecting the various blows form hitting his friend. He had to keep JP safe until he could put the creature on his back again. JP, knowing that Skinny would keep him safe, put all he had into lifting the creature up off the ground.

JP yelled as he finally got the creature up off the ground. The creature weighed more than anything JP had ever encountered before. It did not matter though; he had the will and the power to do what he had planned. JP gripped the creature even tighter as he bent backward. The weight of the creature hastened the maneuver, crashing its head into the dirt. Again, the cloud of dust flew into the air, blocking the sight of the three fighters.

The dust settled after a second, revealing the ending to the climatic maneuver: JP, still bent over in a bridge position, held the creature with all his might, preventing it from standing. Skinny had leapt onto the chest of the creature, again preparing to strike the final blow. His swords were steady as he hunched over the face of the creature. The once-red glow no longer emanating from the eyeholes of the helmet it wore, Skinny smiled as he brought his swords down.

A split second before Skinny could strike his blow, laughter emanated from the creature. The red glow flared like a rekindled flame within the helmet. "Still not good enough, lads!" The creature gripped both of Skinny's hands with one mighty fist, its other hand pushing off the ground on its left, rolling it and JP over. The creature, still holding Skinny, stood up, placing one heavy boot in the middle of JP's back.

"I must say you two did do better this time, but sadly, still not good enough." The creature looked down at the struggling JP. Its eyes flared once again almost as if it were thinking of how to kill the two men.

JP returned the creature's gaze as he tried to shrug of the creatures' heavy boot. It was no use though; the weight of the creature was too much for him now. He had used all his strength to flip the creature over; he couldn't help but think of it as being a mistake. "You kill us, and it does nothing," JP snorted, sending a cloud of dust into the air, making it obvious that he would defy the creature to the end.

"Oh, but on the contrary, lad. If I kill you two, then my real target will surely come to me." Again, the red lights within the helmet of the creature flared, brighter this time than before, signaling the anticipation of the fight to come. "First, though, I have to make sure that he knows what is happening to you two." The creature allowed Skinny to free one of his arms.

Skinny hadn't realized at first that the creature had allowed him to free his hand. Without thinking, he began to strike at the creature furiously. However, with each blow, there was only the steely clink of metal, telling Skinny he could do nothing. The creature allowed Skinny his futile attempt to free himself for only a second before grasping Skinny's arm with its other hand.

"Now, now, that is enough. Instead of wasting your precious energy, how about you send your master a message for me." The creature cocked its head to one side as it spoke. As if curious to see how Skinny would respond.

"Bite me, bitch." Skinny glared at the creature defiantly; there would be no way that he would leave JP here to die so he could deliver this creature's message.

"Oh, I have no plans on biting you at all. Also, I would like to inform you that you will be sending the message just not the way you thought I meant." The creature looked down at JP as he spoke. "Actually, both of you will be telling him exactly what I want him to hear." With that, the creature began to pull on the arms of Skinny at the same time it began to press down on JP.

The two men, knowing what the creature was wanting of them, steeled themselves, refusing to scream. Slowly, the creature applied more and more pressure to the two men. JP could hear the metal of his armor began to crinkle under the weight of the creature. It would not take long for it to crush his ribcage as well. He could also feel parts of his armor beginning to stab into his chest. It did not matter though; he would not give into this monster.

Skinny refused to close his eyes or look away from the eyeholes of the creature's helmet. He swore to himself that he would bite off his own tongue before this creature would get him to scream. He felt the straps of his armor break as the creature pulled his arms away from his body. He knew what was going to happen. Slowly, the creature would pull his arms from his body. Still, no matter what, he would not scream; he would not give in.

The two men prepared themselves for a brutal death by the hand of this monster. They knew that Kravin would not do anything as long as they did not scream. They had spent so many years with him, Cher, and Dawg. They both wished they could thank Kravin for taking care of them and Cher for training them. It was at this moment that Skinny saw it.

A flash of light came from somewhere off to his left. The light crashed into the face of the creature with a high-pitched clank. JP, hearing this, instantly looked up to see what was happening. At first he thought that maybe the creature had managed to remove one of Skinnys' arms. Instead, he saw a dagger attached to a length of chain being pulled away from the creature. He had seen this before, but given the circumstances, he could not remember exactly when or where.

Skinny too saw the dagger, instantly he followed the chain to see where the attacker was. He was shocked to see a girl standing on the edge of the circle. Her hair was short and dark; he could not help but think that her beauty was rivaled by only a few in the world. Her skin was tan from what he could tell from her legs. Her upper body was shrouded in a shawl and shoulder armor.

Each of her fists were covered by gauntlets, each extending down her forearm. He could see that the chains attach directly into the gauntlets. He had heard a story about something similar to this before. The pain from his arms though prevented him from being able to recall just where he had heard this. It did not really matter though. She had managed to throw the creature off balance; the creature stepped off JP and dropped Skinny to the ground.

"Get the hell out of here!" was all Skinny could shout before the pain of his wounds finally caused him to black out.

261

CHAPTER 23

The girl who had attacked the creature moved into the opening of the battlefield. Her face was painted with anger as she glared at the creature. The dagger that had struck the creature now rested in her hand, the chain retracted into the gauntlet somehow. Her movement was musical to say the least as she moved. Though the girl was in the middle of a battlefield, it was as if she were dancing while she walked.

"Well, lass, let me ask you a question? Might you be associated with these two as well?" The creature returned the look of the girl as it spoke. At the same time, the creature simply opened its hand, causing the axe it had dropped to come flying back.

"Well, if they fight for the Garden, then I guess I might. To top it off since you are trying to kill them and I am trying to kill you, would also mean I just might be associated with them. Truthfully though, I have never seen either one of them outside of this battlefield." The girl smirked as she spoke to the creature, as if toying with a child.

"Well, I say don't you have a mouth on you." The creature moved its head back as if offended by the girl's sarcastic tone.

"Yeah well, my mom says I got it from my dad. Everyone else says I am just like my mom. Which would mean I am the best of both of them, wouldn't you say?" The girl posed for a second as she finished her statement. Her eyes never left the creature though; something about her also made it clear she was ready to fight.

"Oh well, if that is the case, let's see just how good your parents are, shall we? Once I am done doing that, I will get back to my more important matters." The creature kicked both Skinny and JP off towards the side of the circle as it hefted its huge axe.

"Oh well, that is all nice and stuff but—" The girl, not finishing her statement, flung out one arm, sending her dagger flying at the creature. The creature quickly moved its axe between it and the dagger, deflecting the blow, only to hear the clank of metal on metal as her other dagger struck the creature in the side. "I have no intentions of letting you get away."

"My, my, someone put a lot of effort in making you pretty good there, little girl. Well, I guess I will bite then. I do not plan on holding back though, so I suggest you do the same." The creature, for the first time since encountering JP and Skinny, raised its axe, taking a battle stance.

The dagger and chains of the girl did not retract this time into her gauntlets. Instead, they hung a foot down from her hands, rhythmically swaying as the girl rocked on her heels. The two stood staring at each other for what seemed like hours; in reality, it was only seconds, each one looking for an opening in their opponent's defense.

The girl knew already that the armor that covered the body of the creature would not be penetrated by her daggers alone. She had to strike the weakest points of the armor in hopes of shattering it. Though she shook her head as she realized she was getting ahead of herself. The first thing she had to do was get past the giant axe the creature was wielding. Slowly, she began to twirl the chains, turning the daggers into makeshift blenders.

"Well, lass, let's not take all day. Although I am curious about something. I know all about the woman who used weapons like those. The only thing is I know you are not her since she was much older than you even back then. So just who are you and how do you know how to fight with those things?" The creature lowered its guard for just a second as he finished speaking.

Instantly, the girl seeing, her opening swung out her arm, sending her right dagger flying at the creature. The creature reacted quickly, moving the head of the axe to deflect the blow. Instantly, the creature jumped high into the air, avoiding the second dagger. The girl moved quickly, retracting her right dagger, rolling out of the way as the creature came down on the spot she once stood.

She spun like a dancer as she flung her left dagger and chain toward the leg of the creature, hoping to entwine it. The creature, shoving its axe handle into the ground as Cher had done, flipped into the air, avoiding the grapple. As soon as the creature touched the ground, it crouched, spinning on one heel. As it did, it held the axe head out far from its body, hoping to catch the girl.

The head of the creature's great axe passed within a fraction of an inch as the girl leaned backward, avoiding the blow. The clink of her dagger returning to her gauntlet rang through the air. The girl, hearing this, flipped backward, again throwing out one of her daggers at the creature. This time, however, it was not met with a clank but a thud as the dagger stuck.

Both the girl and the creature stood frozen as the shock of what had just happened set in. The creature, seeing the dagger sunk in between the plating of its monstrous thigh, growled in contempt. Instantly, the creature grasped the chain attached to the dagger. With a mighty yank, the creature caused the girl to come flying toward him. It readied its axe as it watched the girl with burning eyes.

The girl, instantly triggering the chain to retract into her gauntlet, pulled herself toward the creature faster than it had expected. The girl spun in the air, landing a kick to the side of the creature's head. Instantly, she somersaulted away from the creature, giving her chain a quick yank in order to release it from the creature's armor. The girl landed a few feet from the creature, rolling back in order to get some distance.

"Well, lass, that was unexpected. It would seem as though you managed to get your dagger to stick." The voice of the creature was full of contempt as it spoke to the girl.

"Yeah well, that was just step one, now that I know I can make you bleed. It isn't that much farther to make you dead now, is it?" The girl placed one hand on her hip as if knowing it all the along.

"Oh, on the contrary, lass. I never said you hurt me, I just said you managed to get your dagger to stick. If you take a good look, neither your blade nor my armor has a single drop of blood on them." The creature lowered the handle of its axe to the ground once again. As if to say the girl was not as worthy an opponent as it had hoped.

The girl quickly glanced at the dagger she had just pulled from the armor of the creature. Surprise flashed across her face as she saw that the creature was not lying. There was no blood on the dagger. Instantly, she looked, zeroing in on the spot where the dagger had been stuck. Again, there was no blood where she knew there should have been.

Anger surged through her as she realized that she had not yet figured out a way to stop this creature. Instantly, she moved, spinning to her left, allowing one of her daggers to fling out from her hand. The dagger whizzed through the air as it flew toward the creature. This time, however, the creature did not move all that much. Simply tilting its head, the creature allowed the dagger to go flying by.

The girl did not waste time waiting to see if her first attack had worked. As she stopped her spin, she pulled the dagger back, throwing the other one at the face of the creature. The once-rhythmic dance of the girl was now nothing more than a violent attempt to strike a blow against the creature. A blow that would bring blood pouring forth from a wound. Again, the creature barely moved, stepping slightly back with its left foot, allowing the second dagger to fly by.

"Well, lass, this was fun and all, but I do have things I need to get back too." The creature squared itself with the girl as it waited for the next attack.

The girl, never responding to the creature, sent yet another flurry of blows flying through the air at the creature. The creature simply knocked the first attack away, sending the dagger flying off to the side. Instead of deflecting the second, it instead hooked the chain of the dagger. This caused the dagger to spin around the handle of the great axe.

The girl, realizing that she had just been trapped, desperately jerked at the chain, trying to unhook it from the handle of the axe. It was no use though; she could not get it to unhook. The creature mildly shook its head as it looked at the girl. Fear crossed the girl's face as she realized the creature had her now. There was nothing she could do to unhook herself from the chain that was now wrapped firmly around the handle of the creature's axe.

The creature gave the axe a quick jerk, sending the girl hurtling toward it. The girl flew through the air, unable to stabilize herself. She blinked as the sky and the ground spun around her. Suddenly, it all stopped as the boot of the creature landed firmly in her gut. The air was pushed from her lungs, leaving her gasping for breath. As the girls vision steadied, she could see that the creature had raised its axe, ready to bring it down and split her in two.

The girl, realizing that this would be the end of her life, allowed a few tears to stream down her cheeks before closing her eyes tightly. She did not know how to deal with this situation, and all she could think was that she did not want to see the blow coming. For a second, the light that was shining on her eyelids, then it disappeared and came back again. She heard the creature grumble in pain and the clanking of metal. It was the smell that brought her back from her terror—that wet dog smell.

CHAPTER 24

Kravin stood watching as his friends fought the creature at the head of the Oritha army. He stood watching JP and Skinny fight for all they were worth to try and kill the metal monstrosity. His eye moved with every flick of Skinny's swords and massive blow from the axe of the creature. In his mind, he was screaming at the two, trying to tell them what they should and should not do.

When the creature had bested both of the two men, his heart sank. It was bolstered, however, as Cher stepped into the circle of fighters. Kravin knew that there would be no way Cher would lose to such a monster. She would take this creature down with just a little effort.

Soon, this battle would be over, and the Garden would be safe.

He grinned evilly as he watched Cher and the metal monster exchange blows. As he had thought, Cher would be able to defeat the juggernaut. Then, though, he slowly began to see that his hopes were for nothing. He could see Cher beginning to slow down and her movements becoming slightly less accurate. Fear gripped him as he realized that she had exhausted herself fighting the Oritha.

He watched as the creature took the halberd from her and tossed her in the air. Instantly, he sent his mind to Ta, screaming at her to get Cher. He knew what was coming and sent Ta to the spot she needed to be. Even with that, it did not relieve the panic as he watched the creature hit Cher, sending her flying through the air. His tempered flared as he saw his dear friend beaten.

Quickly, he turned as Ta teleported both her and Cher to the top of the wall. Using all of his will, he kept his emotions from making him look foolish. In his mind, though, fear gripped him. How would they stop this creature if Cher could not defeat it? He could do it that, he knew, but at what risk. He turned to size up the creature, watching as JP and Skinny again moved to square off with the creature.

272

"Kravin, don't do it. If you go out there, you are doing exactly what it wants." Cher pleaded with Kravin as Katie began to heal her wounds.

"What do mean by that, Cher?" Katie only glanced at Cher, concentrating as much as she could to heal Cher as quickly as possible. "This is going to hurt when the bones reset themselves, so sorry."

Cher winced in pain as the bones moved in her chest. "The thing knows all about you, Bear, and Destriga. It wants to draw you out, Kravin. Whatever happens, you cannot go out there." Cher looked pleadingly at Kravin as she lay on the ground of the tower.

All three men turned their attention to the creature that stood on the battlefield. How could this creature know about them and where did it get its information? Where did it come from and what exactly was it? Were all questions running through the minds of the men. Kravin quickly turned to Cher, ignoring the creature. "Katie, will she be OK?"

"Yeah, she will be fine, but I doubt she is going to be doing any more fighting today." Katie did not move from the woman's side. "Kravin, give me your jacket."

Kravin turned, looking at Katie, puzzled. He did not understand as to why she would want his jacket. His eyes went wide as he realized the answer to his question. The clothing that Cher had been wearing had been torn from the blows she had dodged and received. Without hesitating, he removed his jacket, handing it to Cher.

Cher turned bright red as she too realized the state of her garments. She took only a second to put the jacket on and button it up. "Someone has to get out there and stop the boys, Kravin. You and I both know that they will not stop fighting that thing until they're dead."

Kravin turned back to the fight that was going on between the two boys and the creature. He watched in horror as the two men had already been beaten. They had the upper hand for only a second, or at least that was how it seemed. His power surged within him as he watched his two friends become nothing more than toys to the creature that had bested them.

Yet this only lasted for a moment. His eyes went wide as he watched the girl emerge from the thick of Garden soldiers that stood surrounding the three fighters. Her dagger flew through the sky at the monster, striking it and knocking it off balance. Kravin twitched for a second as he watched the girl begin to fight the creature. He knew however that there was no way this girl could win. "Dawg!"

The man who had been standing watching the battle with the rest did not hesitate as he heard the first part of his name. "On it, bro." The man leapt over the group, flying of the side of the wall. Kravin watched as Dawg fell from the top of the wall. He landed with a huge puff of dust flying up around him. Yet it did not get a chance to settle as the man began to run out toward the spot where the girl and creature were fighting.

As Dawg ran through the crowd of soldiers and Oritha, his speed increased. At first he ran as quickly as any runner but his acceleration never slowed. Soon he ran faster than any human could. At the same time he slowly began to change. His once tanned skin now covered by a coat of fur. His face looked like a wolf with fangs as long as any human finger.

"Do you think he will make it?" Katie had moved up beside Kravin as they both watched Dawg running across the field of battle toward the two fighters.

"Without a doubt. What I want to know is, what is she doing at the front lines?" Kravin turned to face Cher as his anger flared.

"That has nothing to do with me. She was in the reserve as you wanted. She is the one who disobeyed orders and moved forward." Cher leaned heavily on part of the wall, yet her attitude had not diminished with her wounds.

Kravin turned back as he watched Dawg close in on the two fighters. Katie, who had taken his arm, felt Kravin grip her hand tighter as he watched the battle unfold before them. He had to make a lot of decisions in his life yet this one he did not know how to make. He did not even know where to begin in order to make this decision.

CHAPTER 25

The girl slowly opened her eyes, wondering why the creature had not killed her. What had prevented it from making the strike it had been ready to make only seconds prior? It took her a second for her eyes to adjust to the light. Once they had though, she did not believe what it was that she saw. The creature did not just hold his attack, but it no longer stood over her.

She shot up quickly as she realized that she was spared from the death that she had anticipated. As she stood, she realized rather quickly what it was that had changed the situation so drastically. Dawg now stood between her and the creature. The girl watched as the creature stood, obviously knocked away or thrown by Dawg.

"Hmmmmm, I know you as well. You are the man that stands in the shadows of the man I wish to meet." The creature turned its head, looking at the multiple dents in its armor from Dawg. "I would never have guessed you could exert so much force with your bite."

"Well, it's nice to know I can surprise someone I have never met before. As for me being the guy who stands in the shadows, I hate to break your heart, but I don't stand behind him. I watch his back. It's just easier to do that while being in the back." Dawg snarled at the creature as he spoke.

"Say what you will, dog, but you are nothing more than a beast on a leash." The creature pointed mockingly at Dawg as it spoke.

"A beast on a leash? That may be very well and true, but the reality is the leash is given by me, not taken by him." Dawg lowered his body closer to the ground, as if preparing for an attack.

"You lie to yourself, dog. Even now, you are here doing his bidding. All of you do this so that he may keep his hands from getting dirty." The creature lifted its great axe, preparing for the attack of Dawg.

"You're wrong. He does not want us to fight for him, but we choose to fight anyway." Dawg sneered at the creature, emphasizing the sarcasm in his voice.

"What fools, you all would give your lives for that coward. Well, that is all very well and fine, but you too will die, Dawg. You may be strong, but you are still no match for me." The creature stepped forward as he made his threat to Dawg.

"On the contrary, I am more than a match for you. Sadly though, I am not here to fight you. I am here for the girl." Dawg turned as he finished his statement. He scooped the girl up, tossing her on his back as he ran full speed towards the city. He eviscerated every Oritha that stepped between them and the walls of the city. The girl clung to his back for all she was worth.

The two of them moved faster than any man could run. Dawg was second only to Kravin and the other commanders of the Garden. Though it was true very few knew who or what he was, it did not matter to him. He was not interested in fame, but instead he wanted to keep his family safe. He did not think like Kravin, which was why he decided Kravin was more important than him.

He never slowed as he entered the ranks of the Garden soldiers. It would have been a waste of time if he did. The soldiers all saw him leave the walls of the city, and seeing him come back, they parted. The girl could barely believe the speed at which the two moved. She kept her eyes closed for fear of being startled and falling. Simply because at this speed, it could be fatal.

When the girl did open her eyes, she quickly realized that she should not have. The two of them were hurtling towards the wall of the Garden, and Dawg showed no signs of slowing down. Fear began to mount as she squirmed. Too afraid to jump from his back yet too afraid to hold on. The two of them were seconds from crashing into the wall as Dawg finally leapt into the air.

The claws on both of his hands and feet dug deeply into the brick and mortar of the Garden wall. Even though they were scaling a wall, it did not cause Dawg to slow any. He hurled them up the wall faster than anything the girl could believe. As they reached the top Dawg jumped into the air above the wall. At the same time he spun and tossed the girl into the air.

As he landed back in his human form, he caught the girl as she fell. Smiling, he placed her lightly on the ground. Everyone atop the wall stood staring at the girl Dawg had just rescued. Slightly confused, she looked around at everyone trying to figure out what had just happened to her. No one said a word until Skinny, who had been brought back by Ta and healed by Katie.

"Man this chick is hot." Skinny stared at the girl in awe. He had barely caught a glimpse of her before he blacked out after fighting the creature. Now, however, he could see just how beautiful this girl was. "But what makes her so special, bro?" Skinny turned to look at Kravin.

Kravin had already been staring at Skinny though. His eyes burned with killer intent. Skinny had never seen Kravin look as he did right now. Even he, with all his crazy talk and giant ego, found himself trembling beneath the gaze of Kravin. "What makes her special is—"

Kravin was cut short as the soft voice of the girl broke the air. "Daddy!" The girl barreled across the wall, tearing herself from the arms of Katie, who had been embracing her. She jumped, gripping Kravin around the neck, her feet kicking the air like a child.

The intensity that had overcome Kravin left him faster than it had taken over him. The man embraced the girl, squeezing her as tightly as he could without causing her harm. The girl whispered to him as she hung from his neck. "You came back."

Kravin did all he could to not begin weeping right then and there as his daughter hugged him. "Yes, I did, but I have to go do something, but it will only take a moment. I promise I will never leave your sight." Kravin set the girl down on the ground as he turned to face the monster that had tried to harm her. The time had come for this creature to meet the man he was trying to meet.

CHAPTER 26

Kravin stood atop the wall, staring at the creature. His eyes filled with the dark red energy once again. This time, however, it flared out from his eyes. His once-torn and tattered clothing no longer showed the signs of age. Instead, they seemed to be almost brand new. Not a single strand or string dared to hang from any seam or hem.

The sun that had graced the battlefield the entire day slowly faded from view. Instead, it was replaced by dark gray clouds. The sky flashed with lighting the same color as Kravin's eyes. The ground trembled, and the air shivered as the thunder boomed after each flash. It was as if the rage of Kravin was being reflected by the environment itself.

The creature stood in awe at what was happening around it. Though it did not seem to be afraid. Somehow it was giving of the vibe as if it had seen things like this before. The creature's eyes flashed back and forth, scanning the horizon for some kind of movement of the man he was desperate to meet. This had to be him; only he would be capable of such power of this scale.

The Oritha all stared at the sky, seeing what was happening. None of them knew what to do or how to act. The sky had changed so quickly that it startled all of the Oritha. It did not take long, however, for the entire mass of Oritha to find something that caught their attention. The metal creature noticed as well what his forces were beginning to look at: Kravin floating in the air directly over the main force of Oritha.

He did not move, nor did he say a word as he floated. His eyes were locked on the creature that had just tried to take his daughter's life. It wasn't until one of the Oritha, who carried a bow, fired an arrow into the sky in hopes of striking Kravin did he finally take any action. His rage had consumed him at this point, and seeing the Oritha arrow come at him but fall short before coming close, it finally pushed him to full action. Kravin fell from the sky, his arms never flailing, nor did he move his legs.

With a crash, he landed the force of his fall so great that it knocked back a huge mass of Oritha and creating a crater into the ground. Kravin turned in a circle, looking at the now-shocked Oritha forces. The once-rage-filled expression was now nothing more than a solemn smile. He turned and faced the metal creature, looking for a way to move through the Oritha that stood between him and his target.

It was obvious that the Oritha would have to be killed in order for him to get to the creature. They were not attacking him, but in their awed state, they would not be able to move on their own. Again, a single brave Oritha jumped to attack Kravin. Its attack was useless against him though; snapping his fingers, the Oritha exploded in midair with the same energy that flared from the eyes of Kravin.

After dispatching the single brave Oritha, Kravin again turned his attention to the creature that awaited him. Kravin raised his hands slowly, and with a clap, the energy surged out in wave. As the wave hit the Oritha forces, they withered and died where they stood. Their deaths quick and quiet; no screams or howls were heard as the masses of Oritha fell. With each one, a stream of that same energy returned to Kravin, being absorbed into his body.

His smile grew wider as he walked past the corpses of Oritha that lay below him. The metal monster, who stood waiting at the end of the path, did not quiver or tremble.

Instead it merely stood, leaning on the handle of its axe, waiting for his opponent. The circle that had been generated from the battle with the creature prior to Kravin's arrival had never filled in. Instead, the Oritha all kept their distance from the metal creature. As Kravin entered the circle, they drew back even farther, fearing the power of the two warriors.

"Well, well, well, if it isn't Kravin, the mighty vampire lord. Finally decided to come do your own dirty work, eh?" The monster chuckled slightly as it stared at Kravin.

"It would appear so, wouldn't it? I must say though it has been a long time since I have been called vampire lord. I am curious, where did you come about such information?" Kravin's gaze never left the creature as he spoke. He knew that after what the Oritha had just seen they would do nothing to try and attack him now.

"Well, that is a secret that I am going to be keeping to myself, thank you. I am curious though, do the nice people of the Garden know just what you are? Perhaps they would be rather interested in knowing their late founder was a demon in disguise?" The creature stood straight as he mocked Kravin.

"Well, I highly doubt that any of them would even remember that I helped build this city. Those who would have are long since dead. As for those who live there now, I would say they probably won't care all that much, considering what is about to happen." Kravin smiled as he imagined the tortures he would love to put this creature through before killing it.

"Oh, and what might that be?" The creature hefted its great axe up on its shoulder as if to say nothing is going to happen.

"Oh well, I plan on killing you. I would like to kill you slowly, but you see, my daughter is watching, and I would hate for her to see just how horrible a creature her father is." Kravin laughed a bit at this though as he spoke.

"Oh, your daughter, is it? You mean the lass that I almost killed until your faithful hound got in my way?" The creature seemed to be interested in the idea of Kravin having a daughter. "Well, now that would make sense. I knew that I heard about that particular style of fighting before, yet that girl wasn't old enough. I assume her mother taught her how to do that, eh?" The monster leaned forward, slightly anticipating the answer to its question.

"Well, as for that, I don't really know. The girl is rather stubborn though. I would have no doubts that her mother doesn't even know she has those weapons of hers." Kravin sneered at the creature in disgust as he spoke of his family.

"Oh well, after I have killed you, I guess I will have to go ahead and take this city. I would love to meet your lovely wife. I have heard it be said that she is like an angel. As for your daughter, I wouldn't mind having her tend to me at my bedside." The creature stepped slightly, widening his stance, preparing for an attack from Kravin.

"Well, if you think she would just let that happen, you are mistaken. Even if you by some grace of God manage to kill me, I assure you my wife will be more than happy to rip you limb from limb. Especially if she hears you speak about our daughter that way." The fingers on each of Kravin's hand begin to grow at this point. Each one growing half again its size, ending in a long sharp point. It was clear to both men that their little discussion was coming to an end.

The creature laughed for a moment as it gazed at Kravin. Both of them analyzing the other, trying to read the movements of their opponent. The creature was the one who chose to move first, dashing at Kravin, raising its great axe over its head. Kravin stepped to his left ever so slightly as the creature brought the axe down. Dust sprang from the ground from the impact. Kravin instantly drove the now talons of his right hand into the side of the creature's helmet.

The force of Kravin's blow drove the creature to roll with his hand. The screeching of Kravin's talons on the metal helmet tore through the air. Again, the creature attacked, swinging with its waist this time. Kravin in turn moved his hands in the way, blocking the blow with his talon alone. They had become just as strong as steel if not stronger.

The battle escalated from here as the two began to fight with all their might. Their movements hastened and their blows stronger. The two monsters seemed to disappear from sight as they fought. Flashes of light illuminated the two as the talons of Kravin met the steel of the creature's armor and axe. All the soldiers of the Garden could do nothing except compare this battle to that of two gods at war.

The battle lasted for several minutes, neither of them slowing. Finally, with a large boom, a huge dust cloud covered the field of battle. None could see what had happened. A minute passed, the dust settled, and a gasp was heard that echoed among everyone and everything that was watching. Kravin and the metal creature stood close to ten feet apart, both of them looking at the other.

Kravin though stood with only his left arm raised. His right arm, soaked with blood, dangled at his side. The creature must have struck a blow that had paralyzed his arm. Yet Kravin did not flee; his goal was not yet met. He simply prepared himself for what was to come.

"Well, I must say, the mighty Kravin lord of the vampires, or whatever you are, you have been a worthy opponent. To think that you could put so many dents in my armor with just those fingers of yours. I am impressed." As the creature finished its statement, it leaned forward, spreading its grip on its axe. The creature twisted its torso to bring the axe back for one final blow.

Kravin never blinked; he did not move. He simply waited for the attack of the creature. Dust exploded from behind the foot of the creature as it lunged forward. Flying through the, air the creature swung its mighty axe at Kravin. Kravin, anticipating the maneuver, moved his good hand to block the blow. Yet the blow that he thought was going to strike his side did not happen.

The creature swung its axe early, causing it to spin in the air instead of landing a blow to the side of Kravin. The creature brought its great axe down overhead. Kravin did not have time to react to the maneuver and watched as the axe of the creature came upon him. The force of the blow brought the axe down, splitting Kravin from head to hip.

The body of Kravin split like a banana as the blade moved through it. His face contorted in shock, and terror stuck on both halves of his face. The creature cackled as it saw the work of its blow. It wrenched its axe free from the body of Kravin and moved past him, looking at the walls of the city. It could not help but feel overjoyed, waiting for the screams of those that cared for Kravin.

The screams, however, did not come. The creature was confused at first. How could those who cared for him control themselves at the sight of what had just happened? Then it struck the creature. Something was not right. It had not paid attention to its surroundings. Quickly, the creature turned to see the body of Kravin still standing where it had struck him.

The creature had not heard Kravin hit the ground. Quickly, the creature moved around the body of Kravin to see why he had not fallen. It was now that the creature saw it. As it looked at the body of Kravin, it could see that his body was not like any other. There were no bones in this man, nor were there organs. His body appeared to be made purely of blood.

The creature stepped back at the sight of this. The red light in the helmet of the creature dimmed as it saw the halves of Kravin's face. The look of terror and panic had disappeared. Instead, his eyes were menacing and a smile started on one half, finishing on the other. The creature could not talk or move as it watched the body of Kravin.

The two halves of Kravin began to change color and flow like a liquid. Soon they were nothing but a red mass of liquid. The blood moved and churned as it pulled itself together. The body of Kravin began to take the shape he had been prior to the blow. It took only a few seconds for Kravin to reform with a smile upon his face.

"I said it had been a long time since anyone had called me vampire lord. I didn't mean because no one knew. On the contrary, a vampire, if they do exist, is nothing compared to me. You spoke as if you knew what I was, but it would seem the one who sent you out here did not tell you everything. I am no vampire. I am something else entirely. Something that my friends and I have aptly named a blood lord." Kravin smirked as he gazed at the now awestruck creature.

Kravin raised his hand, pointing it at the creature. "I have a lot of very interesting abilities. You have seen a few of them, but the best one is yet to come." Kravin flipped his hand over as if pulling the air. "You see, I am nothing more than the blood that I have consumed over my life. Now, though, I do not need blood to survive. Actually, I do not really need anything. I do, however, enjoy a little treat from time to time. That treat is the very life force or essence that all living creatures poses. Of course this information won't matter to you anymore."

Again, that blackish red energy from before began to flow to Kravin, the small strands emanating from the body of the metal creature. Seeing this, the creature franticly tried to sever the strings of energy and remove them from its body. Though it did nothing to stop what was happening. The creature fell to its knees as Kravin drained the life force from it. The monster let out a roar as it finally fell to the ground. Its once-massive armor now crumbled and misshapen.

Kravin smiled as he turned back toward the wall of the Garden. He did not know how the people of the Garden would treat him after seeing what had happened, but it didn't matter now. He had already shown some of his power and just how much of a monster he was, he thought to himself as he moved back towards the wall, ignoring the Oritha that retreated around him. How sweet it was to taste the essence of another creature once again.

As he finally moved out of the ranks of the Oritha, Kravin teleported himself forward to the top of the wall. His daughter, again hugging him with all her might. Tears streamed down her face as she held her father. It did not matter to her one bit that her father could do such things. She loved him just the same because she knew that he had a kind heart that cared for all those around him.

Kravin patted the head of his daughter, consoling her. "Come now, Angelica. I told you I would be right back and that I wouldn't leave your sight."

Hearing this, the girl began to weep, overcome with joy at the thought that her father had come home. That the three of them would be a family once again. She pushed back from Kravin, grinning so broadly that her cheeks began to hurt. She looked at her mother and father, not knowing what to say or how to act. A bark from off in the distance startled her. Turning, Angelica jumped as she saw the large beast pounce.

"OK, OK, Lady, I missed you too." Angelica giggled as Lady licked her face avidly, showing the girl that she too had missed her. She pushed as hard as she could to try and get the large dog like beast of her. It was obvious it would not happen until Lady was ready to move.

EPILOGUE

Katie had been overcome with joy for months. Her husband had returned home, and her daughter was happier than she had seen her in a long time. The Oritha had retreated from the field outside the Garden, but the smoke of fires still loomed on the horizon. Yet still in the past few weeks, she had trouble sleeping.

This was something she had experienced before the flash. Yet it had gone away for so many years. In truth, the only time she would have trouble sleeping was when she was worried about Angelica or Kravin. Everything seemed fine to her now. So why was it that she could not sleep?

Katie had roamed the streets for what seemed hours before she came to the castle. It seemed weird to her that both she and Kravin would always somehow end up here when they had things on their mind. She opened the door and began to move into the dark hallways. She already knew the destination she would end up in no matter what turn she took.

Knowing that, she simply wandered the hallways, thinking that maybe this time it would be different. Yet as she moved, she saw the signs on the hallways and corridors. Her feet were taking her to the balcony that Kravin and she had shared such grand memories at. It didn't matter to her as she stepped out on the balcony, basking in the glow of the moon.

Her memory raced as glimpses of images passed in and out of her thoughts. Memories of a past so long ago she didn't even believe it was real. The day he had proposed to her and the day she had told him she was pregnant with Angelica. It seemed as if she would have given birth to their daughter right here had it not been for Cher making her stay in bed.

Katie thought to herself that perhaps this was the reason she and Kravin always ended up here at this spot. The memories they had were both full of joy, such joy that it could overpower any hardship and sadness. She even noticed that as she stood staring at the stars and the moon that a smile had managed to creep across her face. Maybe she was just being paranoid about the situation.

Yet she could not shake the feeling that something was wrong. Katie just could not put her finger on it.

Finally, Katie decided she had wasted enough of her night on memories and needed to get back and sleep. She knew Kravin would be waiting for her, but he would simply smile as she returned to bed. He did not need to sleep since the flash, yet he still took pleasure in lying next to her as she slept. He had told her once that it was as if everything was back to normal.

Katie passed through several corridors on her way out of the castle. One of which held the only two torches that remained lit at this time. The room that Kravin and the others had created to hold their meetings and discussions. It was also the room that they would use to settle disputes with one another. Destriga, with all his power, had separated the room from this particular plane of existence. Which meant once you stepped through the doors, nothing that happened in the room would affect the castle or people in the city.

Katie moved by the doorway looking at the torches as they burned. Something beckoned to her, as if calling her name. It made no sense to her as she was not very fond of the room itself. Over the years, she had made it a point to try and avoid the room. The fact that it was somehow detached from this reality made her nervous. The fear of being lost within the room was always on her mind.

Yet tonight, the fear was not there. Instead it was replaced with a curiosity. Giving in, she moved to the door and opened it. Passing through the door was something she always thought weird. She expected something like a tunnel of light or darkness which lead to the room. Instead, it was simply this doorway, and the only odd part was that the door would always close behind whoever entered.

It took Katie a moment for her eyes to acclimate to the different lighting in the room. Gradually, she began to see the various shapes of the table and chairs that were set around the fire that burned in the middle. A gasp escaped her throat as the figure of a man stood peering at the fire in the room. "Juerg, is that you?"

"Yes, Katie, it's me." Juerg did not look at Katie though as he spoke. Instead, his gaze was held by the fire that burned in the room. "He used a lot of his power again, didn't he?"

Katie instantly looked at the flames that flared and writhed in the center of the room. Most of the flames were of a natural color. Yet as Katie moved her gaze from the top of the fire to the base worry over came her. The base of the fire was nothing but black and gray now. She had seen it before when Kravin had returned.

Though at that time it did not consume as much of the flames as it did now. Now though a large portion of the flames were black as night. She knew that this was new, that this was because of him using his power. He also meant that things may become very dangerous in the near future.

The Grand Coward

Book 1 of the Garden of Lost Souls

ABOUT THE AUTHOR

Craig E. Hays was born in Wyandotte Michigan in 1983. He was raised in the village of Carleton. After graduating from high school he began a career in automotive. In 2008 he began working on small aircraft jet engines. While training for this he acquired a Bachelor's degree in Animation through Westwood College. His book "The Grand Coward" is his first attempt at writing a novel. He currently lives in the Midwest.